ELLE GRAY | K.S. GRAY

# OLIVIA KNIGHT

### FBI MYSTERY THRILLER

# WHISPERS
## AT THE
# REUNION

# CHAPTER ONE

OLIVIA KNIGHT HELD HER BREATH AS SHE TOOK IN THE scene before her. She watched Jonathan's throat bob as he swallowed, a sheen of sweat coating his forehead, his eyes bloodshot. Behind him, Yara's hand shook as she trained the gun on the back of his skull, her eyes wide with fear.

Then, standing behind Yara was Adeline Clarke, otherwise known to them as The Gamemaster. She was the only one enjoying herself, a youthful smile playing on her lips, glee lighting up her eyes. She looked like a child who had just been offered ice cream on a hot sunny day, not a dangerous terrorist and murderer holding hostages in the middle of the night. Looking at her in any other circumstances, you would never guess what she was capable of. But she was holding a gun too. And Olivia knew that for as long as it was pressed to Yara's head, Yara would do whatever was asked of her.

"Isn't this a sweet little reunion?" Adeline said cheerily. "It's been a while since we were all in a room together. Last time didn't work out quite as I had planned…what with me going to jail for a little while and everyone walking away alive…but hey, it was all part of the fun."

Brock growled and started toward her, but she raised the gun from Yara's head and pointed it straight toward him.

"Ah-ah, Brock," she said sweetly. The smile on her face made Olivia sick to her stomach. "Wouldn't want to do anything you regret, now would you?"

He froze, a deep scowl etched on his face, and his hands clenched and unclenched repeatedly in anger.

Adeline giggled. "You're so cute when you're angry!"

"Shut up!" Brock snapped. Olivia cut her eyes over to him. He was barely holding it together, his eyes dark and clouded with fury.

Not that Olivia herself was doing much better. She, too trembled in fear and rage. She tried to catch Yara's eye, tried to convince her that this was madness, tried to convince her that somehow she could fight back against the monster that held her captive, but the woman was a blank slate.

"How did you get inside?" Brock demanded. "The security protocols—"

The Gamemaster cut him off with a shrill, deranged laugh. She threw back her head and cackled so cruelly, so viciously, that it felt like knives stabbing into Olivia's heart.

"Security protocols? Those little things? Oh, god, you can't be serious." She wiped a tear from her eye. "After everything we've been through, you think I'd let a little FBI security stop me? It was so simple to override your system and plant all sorts of viruses to let me do anything I wanted. And I mean *anything*. All I had to do was walk right into the front door, dispose of the guards, and disable the emergency beacons. You know what that means?"

It was Olivia's turn to scowl. "Nobody's coming for backup."

Adeline laughed again and gently tossed back her golden tresses, shimmering in the darkness. It was so odd to see such a beautiful, brilliant young girl, so consumed by sociopathy and evil. She could have done great things, but instead, she chose to wreak havoc and sow destruction for seemingly nothing other than her own pleasure.

"Very good, Olivia! And now we're here, and I got to catch up with dear old SAC Jonathan James. He slipped away from me last time, but that's not going to happen again. No one will stop me this time. I'm not leaving this room until someone is dead."

"Don't do this," Olivia pleaded. She directed the words at Adeline, but it was Yara's eyes that she caught. Yara's face said it all. She wasn't the confident, beautiful actress she had once been. She was no longer the glamorous movie star Yara Montague. She had been broken down, her face gaunt, her eyes haunted. A shadow of herself. She had been trained to be the Gamemaster's pawn. Now, she would do anything she was told. It was as if the life had been sucked out of her and injected straight into the teenage girl behind her. Slowly, painfully, she tore her eyes from Olivia's.

"I'm sorry, Olivia, but this is the only way I know how to enjoy myself. Nobody ever taught me to play nice," Adeline said with a shrug. "And living life on the edge teaches you that it could all be over at any time. I could be caught and sent right back to prison at any moment. I'm in the middle of an FBI building, surrounded by people who would love to see me behind bars. But for as long as I have this gun, I'm in charge. It's exciting, right? But it also means I have to make the most of my freedom before it all goes upside down. Which is why I think we should have a little fun while we are all back together."

"You won't be going back to prison at this rate. I'll kill you myself," Brock said through gritted teeth. The Gamemaster tsked. "That's not very professional of you, Brock. What will your boss say?" Feigning sadness, she peered at Jonathan. "Probably not much once Yara puts a bullet through his brain."

"Stop it," Olivia said, her voice choking a little. They were backed into a corner here. Any wrong moves and people would die. But watching Jonathan at gunpoint gave her a terrible feeling

3

in her stomach. If The Gamemaster wanted him dead, then he practically already was. She was trying to find a way to calculate his escape and ensure everyone got out unharmed, but Adeline had likely been planning this for months. She'd had all the time in the world to think about how this encounter would go, and she knew how to put herself in charge. Olivia needed time to figure out a solution, but there was none afforded to her.

"Oh, I'll probably stop, at some point," Adeline said lazily. "I'm sure I'll get bored soon. I often do. But first, I want to play my game. And it's my rules, so you should listen carefully." She smiled. "We're going to play Russian Roulette. There are two guns here—mine and Yara's. One of them contains bullets. The other doesn't. Or maybe they both have bullets in…maybe I'm lying. I guess we'll see."

"It's rigged. We all know it's rigged," Brock snapped. "This isn't a game, it's an execution!"

Adeline held up a finger, her eyes bright.

"But for who? For your precious boss? Or for my dearest Yara, my most prized possession?" The Gamemaster mocked, pouting her lip. "We can't know for sure."

"Of course we know," Brock said, his expression hard and angry. But then his face softened. "Why don't we change the game? You let me choose somewhere to point the guns. At a person."

"Brock, no!" Olivia cried out, her heart lurching into her throat. That was a much more dangerous game to play. The Gamemaster rolled her eyes. She seemed to disagree.

"That's a boring game. We all know you'd choose to point it at yourself and play the hero."

"Don't be so sure," Brock said darkly, his glare boring into Yara. A tear ran down her cheek and her gaze found the floor. For a moment, Olivia felt a pang of miserable sympathy for her. This wasn't what she wanted either. But what choice did she have if she wanted to live? She had known this was coming. She'd had so much time to make her choice.

And she was still going to make the wrong one.

"I told you, Brock, we're playing by *my* rules. Either that or I just shoot down every single one of you," Adeline said. The playfulness had left her eyes, replaced by determination. "I'm the one in control here. No one else in this room can rival me. Why would I change that?"

"To make it fair," Olivia whispered. The Gamemaster looked at her and scoffed.

"Fair? Life isn't fair, Olivia Knight. You of all people should know that."

"I do. But I don't go around killing people for fun. My bad luck follows me around because people like you can't get by without killing people," Olivia said, her tone darkening. "But every kill is a choice. Every move and countermove is a choice. You're not too far gone. You can stop at any time. You just choose not to."

For a moment, Olivia thought she saw the young woman's eyes soften a little. She was a broken woman, damaged by her parent's deaths and their cold, secretive lives. She had been raised to follow their dark path. But she was still so young. So full of ideas, full of energy. She didn't need to keep choosing the wrong path.

But Olivia knew she would anyway. The guilt on her face faded as fast as it had arrived, replaced by a cold smirk.

"You're right. I'm choosing this path," she said. "And you're right on a second count. It's not a game if I get to choose the winner every time. But oh well. I guess I'm no Gamemaster. Maybe more of a puppet master. I pull the strings and you dance for me."

"I won't dance for you!" Olivia roared. "Stop this!"

Adeline smiled patronizingly. "Cute." She looked at Jonathan and her face dropped all emotion... "Yara, pull the trigger."

Jonathan made a horrified gurgle, grasping for words that wouldn't come to him. Olivia was frozen in space. If she moved, guns would start firing anyway. Nothing she did would be enough. Yara trembled, shaking her head desperately.

"Not again. Please, not again ..."

"It's you or him," Adeline snarled. She moved closer to Yara's ear. "Remember who pulls your strings, little puppet. You'll die if you disobey. I won't even blink. You know me well enough at this point to know I'm telling the truth."

Yara was panicking. Olivia could see her struggling to find her breath. She imagined being in her shoes, her vision blurred, her brain shutting down, going into survival mode. She knew how tempting it would be to end it all, to pull the trigger, to stop Adeline's cruel whispers in her ear.

"Don't, Yara!" Olivia cried out, but it was too late. Olivia watched Yara's trembling finger move. She saw Jonathan's lip wobble, his eyes slowly closing as he accepted his fate. But, ever the professional, he drew in a deep breath and gave his agents a meaningful, determined look.

"Goodbye, Knight. Tanne—"

The gun fired.

# CHAPTER TWO

NUMBNESS CRAWLED UP OLIVIA'S ARMS AS JONATHAN collapsed from his chair and onto the floor. Her breath left her own body as his did too for the final time. She clasped her hand over her mouth, tears escaping her eyes. Her all-business boss had just died right before her eyes. She began to tremble, unable to take her eyes off his still body.

Yara let out a long wail and Adeline rolled her eyes.

"Oh my god, Yara, stop making that noise. You were the one who pulled the trigger. Surely you knew what was going to happen?"

But Yara didn't seem to hear her. Her entire face crumpled and she let the gun fall from her hands. Olivia turned to see that

Brock's face looked utterly defeated. Olivia could hardly believe what they'd just witnessed. There was no coming back from it.

Everything was different now.

"Stop wailing or I'm going to put a bullet through your brain too," Adeline snapped at Yara. "Pull yourself together. You're going to alert the entire building."

Even in the chaos and fury, Olivia took note of this. So there were some agents still in the building. If only they could find backup… if Yara somehow found the strength to turn against the Gamemaster, maybe they could buy enough time to call for help…

But Yara still didn't respond. How could she? She was clearly in shock. Once again, she had been forced to do the unthinkable against her will. All in the name of survival. But even as Adeline threatened her life now, she didn't seem to care any longer. She couldn't seem to stop the tears. Olivia could feel the ache of Jonathan's loss deep inside her, but she also couldn't bear to watch Yara, crying like a wounded animal. She had been twisted inside, made to do terrible things. But her raw screams reminded Olivia that she didn't want this. She never had. She was being used.

But she seemed to have reached her breaking point. The gun pressed to her head didn't seem to affect her anymore. It was making Adeline impatient. She curled her lip, nudging the back of Yara's skull with her gun.

"Right. You've got three seconds. Three…two…one…"

"Yara!" Olivia cried out desperately. She didn't want to see anyone else die.

But it was too late. Adeline pulled the trigger.

Yara didn't even wince. She had almost accepted it.

But no bullet came from the gun. Adeline laughed loudly, shaking her head.

"Fooled you!" she said, tossing the gun over her shoulder. She pulled another gun from out of her trench coat pockets. "*This* is the real gun. But I'm not about to kill my only leverage, am I? Even after everything she's done, you can't seem to let dear Yara go, can you? Well…maybe Brock can…"

Olivia looked at Brock desperately. His eyes said it all—Yara's actions had cut him deep once again. He'd hoped for better, but he knew not to expect it. At the end of the day, she had been willing to do it to keep herself alive once. She was going to do it again. What else did she have left to lose?

Yara was still sobbing as Adeline grabbed her, pulling her back against her chest. Adeline glanced between Olivia and Brock, breathing hard as adrenaline coursed through her veins. Clearly, she had something else lined up.

"This is how it's going to go," she hissed. "Yara and I are getting the hell out of here, and you're not going to follow us. I hope you're ready for my next game...because somewhere in this building, I've hidden a bomb that will blow you sky high if you can't find it and disable it."

Olivia's heart plummeted to her stomach. Was this another of Adeline's lies? Just a ploy to distract them while she skipped out yet again? Adeline seemed to read her mind, her mouth twisting into a cruel smile.

"You never can tell, Olivia. Which is why you'll go looking for it," she said. "If you don't let Yara and me go, you'll condemn hundreds of people. Yes, that's right. There are still plenty of people in the building. And all of them will die. It's no skin off my nose. I don't mind a little chaos. But I don't think either of you are ready to die yet, and you're certainly not ready to kill a bunch of innocent people. Look what it did to Yara...you don't want to end up that way, do you?"

Anger surged through Olivia. She knew they'd been backed into a corner. Once again, Adeline Clarke was pulling their strings. She was going to get away, and there was nothing they could do about it.

But they could still save everyone in the building. Olivia had no idea how many people were there so late, but she could bet it was more than she thought. And she wasn't willing to let any of them die.

"You don't have long. I could detonate the bomb any time I please," Adeline said casually. "But since you're playing nice,

I'll play fair. Or fairer than usual, anyway. I'm going to go now. I suggest you get searching too."

"We'll find you again," Brock snarled. "You can bet on it."

"Oh, I hope so. I was getting bored of waiting around for you to track us down," Adeline said with a smooth smile. "Besides, I'm not done playing with you yet. This was just the beginning. The real show will begin sooner than you think."

Olivia felt dread twisting inside her, but there was no time to dwell on what Adeline had said. Somewhere in the huge building, there was a bomb that could be about to blow. Olivia held her breath as Adeline brushed past them with Yara in tow, leaving the room. Olivia turned to Brock, shaking with fear and anger.

"I know," Brock said, reading her mind. "But right now, we have to keep our heads in the game. We have to stop another disaster before we can stop her."

# CHAPTER THREE

THERE WAS NO TIME TO WASTE. THERE WAS A BUILDING full of workers who needed to be warned and evacuated. Not just FBI agents, but janitorial staff, administrative staff, all manner of consultants and others. If there really was a bomb, then they couldn't afford to wait around.

"We need to get to the security office and make an announcement," Olivia said, pulling Brock out of the room with her. Her heart wrenched, knowing she was leaving Jonathan's body alone on the floor, but she didn't have time to be sentimental. More people would die if they didn't make a move.

They rushed down the corridor to the security office, bursting in without a second thought. Two security guards were dead on the floor, just as Adeline had claimed. Anger coursed through

Olivia, but she had a job to do. She rushed to the intercom and breathlessly made an announcement.

"This is Special Agent Olivia Knight. Code red. I repeat, code red. There is a threat in the building. Several people have been killed already. We have been informed of a possible bomb somewhere in the building. Please evacuate as quickly as possible. We will track down the bomb."

It wasn't much, but it would have to do. Brock reached over to the emergency alarm and activated it. A loud noise blared throughout the room, drowning out all other sounds. Olivia and Brock left the security office, now faced with an entire building to search and no indication of where they needed to go.

"What's the plan?" Brock cried over the top of the alarm. Olivia wavered.

"Let's split up. We have a lot of ground to cover."

"Okay. I'll take this floor, you should go to the basement and work upward."

Olivia nodded, about to turn and run, but Brock grabbed her arm, his eyes filled with fear. He pressed a kiss to her lips desperately. Olivia forgot what was going on for a moment, lost in his kiss. When he broke apart, he looked even more terrified than he had before.

"Just in case," he murmured.

"I love you, Brock."

"I love you too."

Without another word, they parted. The kiss lingered on Olivia's lips as her feet thundered toward the stairwell. A thousand thoughts were racing through her mind, fighting for attention, but it wasn't the time to be distracted. She hurtled down further and further, heading straight for the basement.

The bottom level of the building was dark and dank, used only for the upkeep of the building, but Olivia wouldn't put it past Adeline to put a bomb in the very heart of the place. She was a little breathless, but she kept running, tossing her head from side to side looking for signs of trouble. She passed through the boiler room and checked the janitor's closet, but there was no sign of anyone there.

She took her search up a level. As she came out of the stairwell, she could see people rushing to evacuate, panicked chatter competing with the sound of the alarm. Agents swarmed the building, just as many trying to coordinate the evacuation as those trying to flee for themselves.

She didn't stop for even a second, knowing that every second counted. She weaved in and out of rooms, doing her best to cover as much ground as she could. But the building was vast and she was sure that they were on a timer. If they didn't find it soon, they would be caught in the blast. There were endless possibilities, and all of them seemed to lead to people dying.

But Olivia refused to watch anyone else die that day.

Her lungs burned as she sprinted through the building. She tried to sort through her jumbled thoughts, wondering where Adeline might place a bomb. Adeline Clarke was a complex woman, leaning into unpredictability to keep them on their toes. It wasn't the first time she had tried to outsmart them. So where would she put a bomb? What would she decide to do if she really wanted to kill them all?

Olivia's thoughts finally slotted into place. Where was the last place someone might look for a bomb? Somewhere private, somewhere that no one would usually open up in normal circumstances. Olivia stopped in her tracks.

Where was the nearest bathroom?

She ran for it. There was one not far from where she had been standing, and she knew in her heart what she would find when she reached there.

The bathroom was silent aside from a quiet whimpering. It was coming from inside a closed stall. Olivia held her breath. Someone was in there.

Likely with a bomb attached to them.

"Hello? Are you okay in there?"

Another whimper followed. Olivia thought the poor person must be tied up and gagged. Olivia moved slowly toward the door. It was locked from the inside, but Olivia knew she could jimmy it open from the slide lock on the door. She scrambled to get it open and the door swung open.

There was a woman tied up and gagged, sitting on top of the closed toilet. Olivia recognized her as a janitor who worked in the building. Tears streaked down the woman's cheeks, and Olivia saw why immediately.

Strapped to her chest was a time bomb.

Olivia took a steadying breath. She would need to stay calm if they were both going to get out of this alive. She didn't know how to disarm the bomb without setting it off. The bomb wasn't very big, but that didn't mean it wasn't powerful. With everyone evacuating the building, her priority was getting the woman out of the bathroom before they both got hurt.

"You're going to be okay. I'll get you out of here," Olivia promised. She stepped closer to the woman, trying to see if there were any triggers that might set the bomb off if she interfered, but it didn't look like it. The bomb was crudely made, the kind that could be made at home by anyone who knew what they were doing. But that didn't make it any less dangerous.

Olivia knew her best bet was to get the woman untied and leave the bomb behind. There was no guarantee that she could disarm it, especially when she had no clue how long she had left to do it. The safety of the woman was more important than destroyed property.

But the bomb was well secured. Adeline had used some kind of strange adhesive to secure the woman and the bomb, along with strong, brown tape binding the woman's limbs. It could take forever to unwrap it from her body, but she had to try.

"I'm going to get you out of the cubicle so I can take the tape off, okay?" Olivia said. The woman nodded tearfully, trembling as Olivia wrapped her arms around her and got her to her feet. She half dragged the woman into the main part of the bathroom, her head pounding from the sound of the alarm, but she blinked past the pain and began to untie the woman. The tape seemed to go on forever—she unwound it as quickly as she could, tearing at the sticky stuff as fast as she could. She was very aware of the bomb sitting right over the woman's heart, knowing that it had the capability to end their lives in seconds. The clock attached to the bomb ticked closer to the hour, but Olivia had no idea what

WHISPERS AT THE REUNION

time the alarm was set to. She just had to hope she had more time than she thought.

"You're okay," Olivia assured the woman, sounding more confident than she felt. She took off the gag binding her mouth. "What's your name?"

"K-Kendra," the woman stammered. "Kendra Dorsey."

"I'm gonna get you out of here, Kendra. We just both need to stay calm," she said, more to calm herself than even to assure Kendra.

She was around halfway through the spool of tape. It was strong stuff, occasionally getting stuck and making Olivia's heart flail, but she didn't stop. If she did, it would be like giving up.

If she did, it would be a death sentence to them.

The sound of a door opening behind her made her heart jolt, but when she saw Brock's face appear, relief flooded through her. At least she wasn't alone now.

"Oh god," Brock said, shocked by the scene he'd walked in on. "Are you okay?"

"We're okay," Olivia said, not stopping. She was near the end of the impossibly long tape. "We need to unstrap the bomb from her and get out of here. You should go and oversee the evacuation. I've got this."

"Of course. You've got this," Brock said with a confident nod. Olivia watched him go, but never faltered in her task.

She was at the heart of the issue now. Kendra was sweating profusely as Olivia was almost at the end of the tape. She didn't want to move the bomb right away in case there was something she had missed, a trigger that might set it off. She placed a hand on the woman's shoulder.

"I just need to make sure we're not going to set this thing off when we unstrap it. Okay? You're doing great."

Kendra nodded, silent tears rolling down her face. Olivia inched closer, her heart racing. The tape obscuring the clock face was stopping her seeing when the alarm would go off. Olivia gently felt around the tape, searching for any other kind of trigger, but there was none. It was time to take the rest of the tape off. With one final pull, she unmasked the bomb.

There was one minute left before the alarm.

"Go!" Olivia cried, yanking the clock away from the woman's chest and lobbing it to the other side of the room. She pulled Kendra toward the door and the two of them began to barrel toward the front entrance. Blood was roaring in Olivia's ears, her hand slick with sweat as she pulled Kendra along.

The explosion hit before they made it to the end of the hallway. Olivia felt it shake the ground beneath her feet, the door to the bathroom bursting open. Shrapnel exploded into the hallway and Olivia threw herself behind the woman to protect her from the blast.

Tile and drywall and concrete exploded out into the hallway, rocking the building's very foundations. Dust billowed and tongues of flames followed them as the ceiling began collapsing.

"Go! Go!" Olivia shouted, her throat scratchy and raw from the dust and smoke already settling around them.

Thankfully, Olivia and Kendra were far enough away to escape the impact, but they weren't out of the woods yet. The building was crumbling behind them, the hallway falling away behind them even as they scrambled for every inch over the debris littering in the hallway. Breathing hard, Olivia looked back. If they had been a minute later...

They found a stairwell and barreled down it as quickly as they could, Olivia praying the whole time that Brock had gotten out safely. Thankfully, despite her terrifying ordeal, Kendra was able to keep her momentum going, and they stumbled out into the lobby and made a beeline for the exit.

Olivia's eyes raced, back and forth, afraid of any last-minute surprises Adeline might have had in store for them. But they couldn't risk waiting, not as the building threatened to come down on their heads and they were only inches away from freedom.

Shaking, Olivia pushed Kendra out the shattered glass windows and then leaped out herself.

Fresh air hit Olivia's face and she finally exhaled. Just like that, it was done. Olivia doubled over, trying to catch her breath, but she knew she'd made it. Adeline wouldn't have had enough time to cause more havoc, she was certain of it. She just needed to create enough of a distraction to get away.

Once again she had slipped through their fingers.

But Olivia was just glad they had gotten out alive at that moment. Kendra pulled her into a tearful hug.

"Thank you. Thank you," she stuttered, her breathing labored. Olivia held her back, swallowing back her tears.

"I'm so sorry you went through that. Let's get you out of here. We'll get you some help."

Brock and Olivia reunited in the parking lot, where chaos was ensuing. The entire place was lit up with lights and sirens. A bomb disposal van had arrived and EMS tended to the injured. Firefighters ran to surround the building even as distressed employees were still rushing away from the building, leaving everything behind. Olivia threw her arms around Brock, finally allowing the tears to leave her eyes. He held her trembling form so tight that it was almost painful.

"You did it. You saved her," Brock soothed her. "You saved everyone."

"Not everyone," Olivia whispered. And only then did reality truly hit her. Jonathan was gone. Yara and Adeline had escaped once again. She had almost died. Everything was wrong.

And Olivia wasn't sure it could ever be fixed.

# CHAPTER FOUR

AFTER ALL THE CHAOS, THERE WAS ONLY SILENCE. IT FELT wrong to be surrounded by it as Olivia and Brock drove back to Belle Grove, war weary and shaken.

Being relatively unscathed—physically, at least—they had been cleared immediately. They had given their statements, and stood around for a few hours as the scene was processed. There was so much more to be discussed, to be investigated—how the Gamemaster had hacked the security of the FBI building, how she'd managed to smuggle a bomb into one of the most secure buildings in the country. They had to chase after her, to find her, to put a stop to her before she took any more innocent lives.

But those were all conversations for later. Everyone—including Olivia and Brock—were far too shell-shocked to even begin to contemplate the next steps. And when dawn crept over the horizon, they had no other choice but to finally make the drive back home.

Olivia hoped Brock might say something to break the moment, to bring some normality back to their lives, but she had a feeling that things would never be quite the same again. Not after everything they had been through.

If Olivia closed her eyes, she would see the moment that Jonathan died over and over again. It was the worst part of it all. Dealing with the bomb should have been worse, knowing that she had been moments away from death, but she knew it wasn't anywhere near as bad. If she had died right there to an explosion, she never would have had time to contemplate seeing her boss who was also her dear friend dying right before her eyes. It would be over in an instant, unlike the pain she was holding in her chest. She had to press her lips together hard to stop herself from crying out. She stared out of the window, trying to concentrate on breathing through the hurt. It had started to rain, and it felt appropriate.

Yara had done this. That was the other thing haunting Olivia. Of course, it was really Adeline, forcing Yara's hand, but Yara had still made the choice to pull the trigger. Again. Back on the island, when she was going through withdrawal, when survival seemed more desperate, Olivia almost understood. But now? It felt even more wrong. After everything Yara had done, everything she had been through, she still made the selfish decision. And for what? What kind of life could she live now? She'd never be free again.

Olivia knew that it was an impossible choice—to choose between your own life and someone else's—but she still felt sure that she would have chosen differently. It was impossible to know for sure, but Olivia had been willing to give her life for someone else before. Strangers, even. In Yara's shoes, Olivia would have considered it her one chance at redemption.

And this wasn't the first time for Yara. She had been making bad decisions for so long now that there was very little room left to forgive her. Olivia had spent months trying to get Brock to consider forgiving her actions, knowing that she had been very sick at the time she messed up, but there was no chance of that now. This had become more personal than they could have predicted. After all they had seen, after all Yara had done, there was nothing left to do, but hold on to their anger. It rattled around inside Olivia like a pinball, making sure she felt the pain in every inch of her body.

When they arrived home, Olivia shuffled slowly inside, allowing the cold rain to lash at her skin and soak her to her bones as she walked. It felt good to feel something other than the gaping hole in her chest. The door had barely closed behind her when Brock pulled her close to his chest, holding on to her for dear life. Her throat closed up, a lump sitting there as she tried not to cry. But the more she held it back, the more she welled up. After a moment, she let the sob escape, and she felt a tear drop fall on top of her head. It wasn't weak to cry. After everything they had been through, it was time to let it go.

Olivia's body shuddered as she cried. There was no way to unsee everything they had experienced. And as Olivia let out her pain and her anger, she made peace with the fact that her life would never feel quite the same again. And Brock, too, shuddered and sobbed right there with her.

So much betrayal. So much death. It was a life they had trained for, a life where they learned to expect the worst. And yet when the worst-case scenario came knocking, they couldn't truly be prepared for it. She should have seen it coming. They had known it wasn't over between them and Yara. But she had hoped for more, and it made the shock of it all so much worse.

Olivia clung hard to Brock. He was her anchor, keeping her grounded even as she lost control of her emotions. She didn't dare let go. So she stayed there with him for a long time, the both of them mourning the people they had been earlier that night. They were dead and buried now. It was time to start over again with fresh wounds that would refuse to close for a long time.

Olivia wasn't sure how much time passed before they drew apart. She looked up at Brock and saw that his eyes were red raw, tears streaked on his handsome face. She reached up to cup his cheek, swallowing down the pain.

"I'm so sorry," Olivia whispered to him. He closed his eyes and nodded once, pain written all over his face.

"Me too," he murmured. "I can't ... I can't believe she ..."

Olivia nodded firmly. She didn't want to make Brock say it out loud. Yara had stuck the knife in Brock's back a long time ago, but now, she'd made the final twist. Olivia knew there was no coming back after what they had seen her do. Yara likely knew it too. Olivia tried to imagine what she was thinking at that moment, back on the run with one of the worst criminals in the country. She could never have pictured her life going that way, surely? But she couldn't escape it now, not even if she kept running for the rest of her days. If they saw her again, things would be very different. There was nothing that could make them forgive her now.

"We should try to rest," Brock said. "Who knows what tomorrow will hold."

Olivia glanced at the sun now steadily climbing out the window. "Or today," she said, but there was no humor in it. "Let's just face it as it comes."

She slipped her hand into Brock's. Together, they moved to the bedroom, never letting go of one another. They barely made it into their pajamas before they crawled underneath the sheets, pulling the duvet over their heads. Beneath the covers, Olivia felt a little safer, somehow. Like they were shielded from the cruelty of the world. She curved her body against Brock's, feeling his strong arms making a cage around her, keeping her from harm. Only in his arms would she ever sleep again.

Sleep finally took her.

# CHAPTER FIVE

I T FELT WRONG TO HAVE POLICE AT A FUNERAL, BUT OLIVIA knew it was necessary. As she got out of her car, she allowed an officer to pat her down, shortly followed by Brock and Jean. She understood that Jonathan's funeral would be a potential target for another terror attack by the Gamemaster. But after everything that had happened, the least he deserved was a private funeral.

But as Olivia approached the church, she realized that the list of attendees was a little sparse. With her mother on one side of her and Brock on the other, she had expected to enter the church with hundreds of other FBI agents who admired Jonathan had been. But she didn't see many familiar faces there.

As they stepped inside, Olivia saw an older woman in black, her back hunched with age. She clutched a crumpled tissue in one hand, dabbing at her eyes occasionally. Olivia realized in horror that she must be Jonathan's mother. It felt like a stab through the heart. No parent wants to outlive their child, but Olivia gathered that she had to be prepared for that her entire life. It made her think of her own sister, dying far too young. It seemed life had dealt them all a bad hand.

Jonathan's mother saw them enter the church and straightened up a little. She reached out a hand to shake and Olivia took it gently, her eyes swimming with tears.

"You must be Olivia Knight," the old woman said with a decisive nod. "I knew I'd recognize you when I saw you."

"I'm sorry, Mrs. James. I'm sorry I couldn't save him," Olivia choked out. The woman clasped her hand harder.

"You did what you could, I'm sure of it. I always knew my son would lose his life to his job. He died like he lived, after all. And you came to his rescue more than once. You were there when he called you. That's what is important now."

Olivia couldn't find it in her to speak. She swallowed, her throat hurting from the effort of holding back tears. The old woman offered her a gentle smile and then dropped her hand, moving on to the other mourners behind Olivia. Olivia walked further into the church, trying her hardest to hold it together. She always found funerals impossibly hard, and she had attended far too many for a woman of her age. But this time, she felt somewhat responsible. Was there something she could have done differently? Could she have saved him if she had moved faster? She knew logically that there was nothing she could have done. But it didn't make it easier.

She found her way to a pew on wobbly legs. There weren't many people in the others, and she suddenly felt a wave of loneliness, almost on Jonathan's behalf. After all his good work, after the difference he'd made in the world, he couldn't even fill a church with his admirers. Olivia clutched the bench. Too often lately she had seen how lives could end with a ripple, not a bang.

It scared her for the future, and it made the funeral seem even more bleak.

"Don't dwell on it, sweetheart," Jean said, sliding onto the bench beside Olivia and taking her hand. "He didn't feel a thing. And he won't again. He's not around to see his funeral. You don't need to feel sorry for him."

Olivia sniffed. "He had his entire life ahead of him."

"It's like his mother said. He was married to his work. That *was* his life. Can you imagine that man ever retiring? Because I can't. I think in some strange way, this is what he would've wanted. To not have to get too old. To not have to live life beyond his career. Besides, he never recovered from the island. He couldn't have carried on the way he was going. You knew him well enough to know I'm right."

Olivia nodded. Because it was definitely true. Jonathan James had never known how to relax, how to enjoy the smaller things in life. He was all or nothing. They were alike in that way. And now she worried that she would go out the way he had, alone and frightened.

But before Olivia could voice her thoughts, Brock squeezed his way into the pew and took a seat on the opposite side of Olivia. He took her free hand in his and ran his thumb over her knuckle. Olivia swallowed.

Perhaps she wouldn't be alone, at least.

The service began shortly after, and Olivia spent a little time reflecting on the man her boss had been. Stern, serious, unrelenting. Smart, loyal, dedicated. Would it be so bad to follow his lead? Olivia bowed her head and thought about Jonathan. She had been proud to work with him. She'd had good times with him, and they had achieved so much together. That was something to hold on to. Even as the service ended and the curtains were drawn on his life. Even as a slow trickle of mourners left the church in silence, leaving him behind.

There wasn't a dry eye in the room. These people had cared as much as she had. He might not have filled the pews, but the people who mattered had been there to say goodbye. Wasn't that something to hold on to? The world had to keep turning without him.

She said a final silent goodbye as she left the church.

# CHAPTER SIX

OLIVIA CLOSED HER SUITCASE ON THE BED, WITHHOLDING a sigh. A family reunion was the last thing on her mind, but it had snuck up on her this weekend. The reunion had been planned for over six months by her Uncle Mark, a chance for the entire family to catch up at the old lake house they used to visit each summer when she was a kid. The whole thing was excessive, with a whole bunch of them cramming into the lake house for the sake of keeping up the appearance of one big happy family. It had been a long time since Olivia had even seen most of her cousins, and she only saw her uncle and auntie once in a blue moon. She didn't even know what she'd say to most of them beyond banal small talk. But in ten minutes, Brock was due to drive them to the lake house whether she liked it or not.

Things had been different back when she had committed to attending. That was back when her boss was still alive, when the threat of Adeline didn't hang over her head all of the time. It had only been two weeks since Jonathan's funeral and it all felt so raw. Her insomnia had returned with a vengeance, and she was surviving on coffee and the fact that she had been ordered to a month of leave from work to recover from their ordeal at the FBI headquarters. There was going to be a new boss to contend with and a whole new level of stress added to her job. And while she was glad to step away for a while, there was little to distract her from everything. Jean had assured her that the weekend at the lake and a little fresh air would do her good. But Olivia thought it would take a little more to pull her out of her funk.

She felt Brock's arms wrap around her from behind and she closed her eyes, leaning back against him. At least she would be with Brock the entire time. He was better with people than she was, and she knew her family would love him. It was about time he met her extended family, anyway.

But he too wasn't coping well with the hole Jonathan had left in their lives. He was quieter than usual and withdrawn. Olivia couldn't expect him to be any different, but she hoped he might be able to bring some cheer to the weekend. Otherwise it was going to be downright unbearable.

"It won't be so bad," Brock murmured in her ear, kissing her cheek. "You never know. It might even be fun. We can have a few drinks, listen to your cousins bicker, get lost in some family drama instead of our own..."

Olivia smiled at Brock's attempt to cheer her up. She'd told him a bunch of stories about her cousins, Caroline and Caitlin. They were sisters, but they'd always acted like sworn enemies when they were younger. Caroline, or 'Caro', as she insisted as being known, was always the fun one, always getting into mischief, while Caitlin was much more serious, always trying to keep Caroline's feet firmly on the ground. Their opposite personalities always made for good entertainment, but it had been years since she had seen them both, and even longer since she'd seen them both in the same room together. According to her mother, they kept out of each other's way as much as they could, so severe was their rivalry. It would certainly be interesting to see them together again.

"They might have grown up a little since the last time I saw them. And I don't think we can break up sibling rivalry with impromptu games of hide and seek anymore…"

Brock grinned. "No, but we can put a glass of wine in their hands and hope they don't tear each other's throats out… but that would at least be funny…"

Olivia turned to swat Brock. "Don't you be stirring up trouble… tempting as it might be. You and Caro are cut from the same cloth, I swear. Both of you are desperate to stir the pot."

"I think we're going to get along just fine," Brock said with a cheeky grin. "But don't worry. Any mischief will not be directed at you."

"I should hope not. I'm hoping for some peace and quiet this weekend."

"In a full house of Knights? Somehow I doubt you're going to get that."

Olivia groaned and Brock grinned even wider, picking up her suitcase to take it out to the car.

"Chop chop, babe. This weekend won't ruin itself."

Olivia turned and did a final check of their home. She didn't want to return to any nasty surprises, so they'd just installed a new security system. So far, it had been fine, but she dreaded to think what might happen while they were away. She hoped her new doorbell camera would catch anything suspicious while they weren't around to keep an eye on things.

She took a few deep breaths and closed her eyes. *Everything is fine. It's all okay,* she told herself. She had found herself checking in with herself more and more often since the funeral, trying to calm her rising anxiety. It helped in some ways, but she still had fear locked inside her chest, pummeling against her ribcage to try and escape. *Think of the fresh air. Think of a crisp glass of wine and the lake. It's going to be okay.*

She locked up the house and went out to the car before she could change her mind. Brock was already waiting for her in the driver's seat. As she slid in the passenger side, he put a gentle hand on her knee, saying everything she needed to hear without speaking a word. He was letting her know that it was all going to be fine.

"Let's get this party started, right?" Brock said cheerily, turning up the radio as he started the car. Olivia could see the effort he was going to to make her feel comfortable so she forced a smile she didn't feel like showing and sang along to the radio with Brock as he drove. And somewhere along the drive, between snacks and bad jokes from Brock, she began to ease up a little. Maybe this weekend wouldn't be so terrible. Maybe it was actually perfect timing.

As they neared the lake house, Olivia felt a rush of nostalgia taking over. Everything looked so familiar to her, even years after her last visit. There were a few new shops nearby, and more houses had been built up around the area, but otherwise, it was the sight of her childhood. As they drove down the hill to the lakeside, she was surprised by the brief flicker of excitement in her stomach. If she really thought about it, wouldn't it be good to catch up with everyone? It wasn't like she didn't like her family. They had just grown apart. Things had been hard on all of them in the years since Veronica's death, even the extended family.

She imagined seeing Caro again—she had always been her favorite cousin. Now that they were all grown up, maybe they could connect again. Olivia had friends here and there, but she knew she could stand to be a little more sociable. Maybe this was a chance to do that.

*Don't get too close to anyone,* the voice in the back of her head sneered. *Everyone you love gets hurt eventually.*

Olivia squeezed her eyes shut. She couldn't shut out those negative thoughts entirely, but she could push them to the back of her mind where they belonged. This had nothing to do with the Gamemaster or Jonathan or any of her other troubles. This was a secluded family retreat. It was safe. There was nothing to be scared of.

But the doubt stayed with her as Brock pulled into the dirt driveway. At least only her parents seemed to be there—theirs was the only car parked up already. Olivia was glad for a bit of time before the chaos began. She didn't imagine there would be a single moment of quiet again until the weekend was over.

She took a deep breath and got out of the car. The air was cool and crisp and she breathed it in, hoping it might work a miracle on her anxiety. It didn't, but it was pleasant. She heard the crunch of footsteps and looked up to see her mom appearing from around the side of the house. She opened her arms to Olivia and she went to her, nestling into her mother's neck for a hug. In recent months, she'd felt closer to her again, her heart finally having healed from her mother's disappearance. Now, she found herself craving her mother's company once again, and the comfort she offered. She closed her eyes and Jean kissed her cheek.

"How are you, darling?"

As they pulled apart, Olivia opened her mouth to speak, to express what was going on in her mind, but her words lodged in her throat. Tears pricked her eyes. It was all too much. But Jean seemed to understand. She pulled Olivia back in, holding her tight in her arms.

"I know these last few weeks have been hard. I know that it feels impossible to enjoy yourself right now, given what you've been through. But you should try. You can't live in fear forever. You can't let that vile woman win."

Olivia nodded, but she was still unconvinced. But Jean sensed that too and took Olivia by her shoulders, fixing her a stern look.

"Listen to me, sweetheart. We're going to let go this weekend. We're going to relax."

Olivia scoffed, but Jean smiled kindly.

"Don't worry about it. You've got me here to keep an eye on things. You don't need to stress. You know logically that we're in the middle of nowhere, that we're safer here than anywhere. That's partly why I insisted that you come this weekend, but I know you didn't want to. But it'll be good for you. I'm not going to let anything ruin this. Any sign of trouble and I'll spot it. Alright? You know you can trust me."

Olivia nodded, feeling the knot in her stomach unravel a little. She felt like a child again, relying on her mom to make everything feel okay, but wasn't that what mothers were for?

Besides, Jean had some making up to do for all those years she was absent in her childhood, putting work above all else. If she was willing to sacrifice her weekend to make Olivia feel comfortable and safe again, then she wasn't going to argue. It was nice for someone to try and lift the burden for her shoulders, even if only for a while.

"Okay," Olivia said quietly. Jean smiled, patting her cheek.

"Okay, good. Your father's out back setting up the grill for tonight. Why don't you and Brock head inside and pick out a room? Mark said it's first come first served...you'd better get the best room before Caro and Caitlin arrive and start fighting over it."

Olivia laughed. The sound was a little uncertain and unconvincing, but it made her feel a little better.

"I'll get the bags then," Brock called from the car, the entirety of their luggage draped on his various limbs. Olivia exchanged a glance with her mom and they giggled. Trust Brock to be able to lighten the mood. Olivia relieved him of a few bags and they headed inside to unpack.

The lake house hadn't changed much. It was like taking a walk through her own childhood memories. It was a comfort to Olivia. By memory, she found the double room at the end of the upstairs corridor, the one beside her uncle's room. Aside from his room, it was definitely the best one, usually reserved for her cousins to share. It overlooked the lake, the calm ripples of water a welcome sight to Olivia's weary eyes. She allowed her shoulders to relax as she put her suitcase down.

For a moment, it felt like coming home.

# CHAPTER
# SEVEN

OLIVIA'S FAMILY BEGAN TO ARRIVE IN A SLOW TRICKLE. She felt a strange sense of nervousness when she heard the first car pull up on the driveway, the slamming of the car doors followed by the familiar sound of her cousins arguing over something stupid. She turned to Brock with a nervous smile and he put an arm around her shoulders, steering her away from the safety of the bedroom.

"It's going to be okay," he murmured in her ear. She nodded decisively. She made the decision to believe him, and that made heading downstairs much easier.

The family burst into the lake house with a cacophony of noise. Caro led the way, tall and slim and beautiful as always. She had cut her hair to align with her sharp jaw and had dyed it platinum blonde. In her wake, Caitlin followed, fury burning her cheeks. She was almost a head shorter than her sister, but just as beautiful, though her dark eyebrows knitted together and creased her lovely face.

"You just swan around like everyone should treat you like a princess," Caitlin was saying, venom spitting with each word. "Can't you just pretend for one day that you're not a complete narcissist?"

"Sorry. Tried that before. That's boring," Caro replied smoothly. Indeed, as she did, she stepped into the center of the living area as if it was her stage and everyone else was her adoring audience. She caught sight of Olivia at the base of the stairs and her eyes lit up.

Olivia pasted on her best smile, trying to ignore the eternal argument. "Hey, ladies."

"My God, Olivia! You got so gorgeous!" Caro said, rushing to her and sweeping her off her feet. Olivia had forgotten her strength—she had often picked her up when they were kids, whirling her around as though she was light as a feather. She found herself laughing, clinging to Caro in a half embrace and half attempt to ensure she wasn't dropped to the ground.

"Well, *I* think you were always gorgeous," Caitlin said as Olivia's feet found the ground.

Caro didn't try to hide it when she rolled her eyes. "I'm sure you remember Caitlin exactly as she is now...she's still got a massive stick up her butt."

"It's good to see you, Cait," Olivia smiled, moving to hug her before the pair could start arguing again. She heard Cait huff quietly, but she returned the hug stiffly before pulling away and gesturing to a man in the doorway to the lake house.

"This is my boyfriend, Finn," she said. Finn stepped forward to shake Olivia's hand, ducking a little beneath the low doorway. He was as tall as Brock and somehow even wider. He wore a football jersey and a baseball cap which should have made him look younger, but somehow aged him. He kept his hair short beneath the cap and he had a ghost of stubble along his jaw.

"Hey. Caro has been yappin' about you the whole way..."

"After we had to pick her up," Caitlin jabbed. "Can you believe she doesn't have a car at this age, Olivia?"

"I prefer to be chauffeured around," Caro said, never missing a beat. Olivia could see she had become acquainted with Brock already, one of her long arms wound around his shoulder in a friendly manner. Caro always did have a way of making friends with everyone she came across. Aside from Caitlin, everyone adored her. "Besides, we haven't seen one another in over a *year*, Caitlin. I thought you'd be pleased to share some quality time."

"I'll get my quality time when you leave," Caitlin muttered, but not loud enough for Caro to hear. No doubt Caitlin had learned over the years that Caro had a comeback for everything if you gave her a chance. Olivia briefly felt sorry for her cousin, but the last thing she needed was to get wrapped up in some sisterly squabbles.

"This is my partner, Brock," Olivia said, gesturing to him across the room.

Caro frowned. "Like your work partner? Come on, he's way too cute for that."

Olivia blushed a little. "Well, yes, he's my work partner, but we're also…you know. Together."

That lit up her face and she pointed cheerily. "Good choice, Olivia! I was just about ready to make my move on that hot stuff."

Brock, for his part, smiled politely. "Sorry, but this hot stuff is spoken for." He broke out into a wolfish grin. "But feel free to keep feeding my ego. It's so hungry."

"I thought that was your stomach," Olivia jumped in. Caro tipped back her head and laughed loudly. Olivia held back a smile. She had known they would get along, and it was pleasant to see them laughing. But when she turned to see Caitlin's cold expression, she knew they'd need to warm her up a little. She turned to Caitlin with a smile.

"I hope you don't mind, we took your old bedroom…"

"Not at all," Caitlin said bluntly. It sounded like she did mind a little. "It's going to be a madhouse in here. As long as I'm not on the sofa I'll be happy. But I guess someone should save a room for Granny…"

"She can sleep on the floor. I hear it's good for old bones," Caro said with a grin. Caitlin huffed and walked toward the staircase.

"Caro, you're despicable."

"Have you ever heard of a joke, dear sister? Laughter, perhaps? You should try it sometime."

Finn laughed as he followed Caitlin upstairs, catching Caro's eye as he passed her. Olivia felt an uncomfortable twist in her stomach. *Poor Caitlin.* It looked like Finn would rather be in on the joke with Caro than back his girlfriend up. She didn't love the tension that already threatened to cast a pall over the entire weekend. But that wasn't Olivia's concern. *Just don't get involved,* she told herself. *Loosen up. Have some fun.*

"How about a glass of wine?" Olivia asked Caro as her sister disappeared upstairs. Caro's eyes lit up.

"Oh, absolutely. What do you drink? Rose?"

"Always."

"Alright then. Let me get you a glass. Brock, beer?"

"I'll drink anything."

"Great. You guys can be on door duty while I get us set up. Granny is coming tomorrow with Cody, but I think our dad is due with the witch any moment now..."

Olivia smirked. Caro had never made any secret of the fact that she hated their stepmother. While Caitlin had managed to get along with her, Caro made life for Stephanie as difficult as she possibly could. Olivia hadn't really spent much time with Stephanie, but given that she was fifteen years younger than her Uncle Mark and had been through three divorces prior made Olivia a little suspicious of her intentions. Once again, she had to tell herself it was none of her business. Even if they were family.

Olivia and Brock settled down on the sofa just as they heard the sound of another car arriving. Olivia was looking forward to seeing her uncle. It had been a while since she saw him, and he was always a jolly man who made for pleasant company. She headed to the door to greet him and found herself faced with Stephanie walking up the path to the house. She was dressed in money, dripping with designer baggage and a real fur coat. Even her hair looked expensive, blonde highlights making it shine in the sun. She gave Olivia a larger-than-life smile, her red painted lips parting to reveal a set of unconvincing veneers. Uncle Mark had always described her as glamorous, but Caro's preferred word was tacky.

"Oh, Olivia! It's been too long!" Stephanie said, kissing the air on either side of her cheeks. Olivia got a whiff of perfume so strong that it was almost alcoholic. "Your uncle is so looking forward to seeing you. Be a doll and carry my bags upstairs, will you?"

"Here, let me take them," Brock said, rushing forward. "I've been the luggage man today…"

"Oh gosh, what a handsome young man you are!" Stephanie said, pursing her lips as though she wasn't exactly very old herself. Brock raised an eyebrow with a cheeky grin.

"So I've been informed today."

"If you're talking about Caro, please feel free to ignore her entirely. That girl is such a wretched flirt," she said with a sniff. As if on cue, Caro appeared, her fingers magically locking around the stem of four wine glasses.

"My ears are burning," she said, baring her teeth in a fake smile. Stephanie didn't seem concerned about being called out.

"Then perhaps you shouldn't eavesdrop, dear, it'll save you from so much hurt."

"Oh, I wasn't offended. I took it as a compliment."

Stephanie made a face that clearly indicated that she had hoped to insult Caro, but it was a nearly impossible task. It took a lot to ruffle Caro's feathers. Stephanie hooked her bags onto Brock's arm like he was a coat stand and then reached for one of the glasses in Caro's hand, but she pulled it away.

"Ah, these are for our guests. Bottle's in the kitchen."

Stephanie's eyes blazed with irritation, but her face remained stiff and motionless. She gently patted Olivia's shoulder as she swept past her.

"Good seeing you, dear."

As Stephanie left the room, Caro caught Olivia's eye and grinned. She offered up a glass to Olivia which she took.

"I think we're going to have some fun this weekend," Caro said. "Cheers."

"Cheers," Olivia said, feeling herself relax a little. There was so much tension on this side of the family that it almost made her feel more chilled out. At least she wasn't in the center of it, after all. With such a turbulent life waiting for her back home, it was nice to know that no one had their life completely in order.

Before she knew it, Olivia was being swept up in the chaos of it all. Uncle Mark and her father emerged from out back carrying trays full of hot dogs and hamburgers fresh from the grill.

"There you are, kid," said Roger Knight, beaming at Olivia as he set the table.

Olivia smiled. "Here I am."

Olivia's relationship with her father had been slower to mend than that with her mother, if that was somehow possible. Much like everyone in the family, he'd dived headfirst into work after Veronica's death and Jean's disappearance, but somehow even after she returned, he'd remained withdrawn at even the best of times. For Olivia to see a smile—a genuine smile—on his face, came as such a shock that she nearly completely forgot all the rest of the family tension.

If all that came out of this weekend was a functioning relationship with her father, that would be good enough for her.

Olivia hugged him tightly, then hugged Uncle Mark, and then Jean too descended from her bedroom to see her brother. Everyone got up to make their plates, wine started to flow, and even Caitlin loosened up a little once she had a glass of white wine in her hand. Caro nudged Olivia as they congregated in the corner of the room, watching the party unfold.

"I poured her an extra large glass. She needs it," she whispered. "And let me tell you, our relationship is a different story once she's had a drink. But we need to keep an eye on her."

Olivia raised an eyebrow. "Why?"

Caro gave her a conspiratorial smirk. "One glass in and she loses those angry eyebrows she's always sporting. Then by drink two, she can look me in the eye without being overcome with rage. And drink three? Drink three's the best one. That's when she starts to giggle. She's so unserious, honestly. She starts making all these lame jokes and puns like the nerd she is. After drink four she's a bit messy, though. And drink five just means a steady stream of vomit, and no one wants that."

Olivia chuckled. "I mean, it is a party. If no one is throwing up, has it really been a successful night?"

Caro cocked her head to the side with a slow smile. "Olivia Knight...you dark horse."

"I hope you know I'm completely joking..."

"Nah, you've done it now. You've identified yourself as a party animal. Well, that makes two of us. I'm glad you're here, Olivia."

"Me too," Olivia said with a smile, sipping her wine. She was pleasantly tipsy already, and she had to admit it was nice to be around Caro again. She really was easy to get along with, despite what Caitlin and Stephanie might feel about her.

Olivia's eyes surveyed the room, taking in her family. Mark, Roger, and Mark's brother Jared were chatting in the kitchen about Mark's new grill with all the bells and whistles. Jean was catching up with Aunt Heather and her toddler son, Brayden, who obviously wanted to join the young cousins playing in the other room. Brock appeared to be making polite small talk with Stephanie and Caitlin. The others popped in and out of conversation. Olivia remembered most of them but had trouble connecting cousins to aunts and uncles, especially on this side of her family. Hannah, Audrey, Stephen, Devin, and Erik were names and faces that flitted in front of her, but she couldn't quite remember if Erik was Heather's son or Hannah's—a feat made no easier by the fact that the two women were identical twins.

Then Olivia's eyes fell on Finn. She saw that he was looking in their direction, but though her immediate instinct was to look away awkwardly, his impulse didn't appear to be the same. When Olivia looked back again, she saw that his eyeline wasn't actually focused on her, but beside her.

"Mr. Wandering Eyes," Caro whispered, hiding her mouth behind her hand as she looked back at Finn. "I don't know how Caitlin doesn't see it. He's totally staring at you."

"I think he might be looking at you, actually," Olivia murmured. Caro raised an eyebrow.

"He stares a lot. I think he's just one of those guys, you know? Always looking for an upgrade. Not that he can do better than Cait. Damn, that sounds bad...I mean she's a catch, and he's... well, he's there. He's punching above his weight, don't you think? And he's kind of immature. I don't see how Caitlin would suit him. She's so serious about everything. Always has been."

Olivia didn't want to gossip, but she had to admit that she agreed with Caro. Caitlin had never tried to be anything but the kind of woman who made you feel guilty for being imperfect. She was judgmental to the point of rudeness at times. And yet if what Caro was saying was true, she had chosen to be with someone who was the complete opposite. From the hungry look in his eyes, Olivia thought he seemed like a man running on impulse, even if it got him in trouble. His gaze on Caro was starting to get a bit creepy.

"Caro, he's definitely looking at you. It's...it's weird."

Caro waved it off. "I know weird men, Olivia. He might be a creep, but he's harmless. He's just looking. He knows he won't get anything from me."

"Don't you think you should say something to Caitlin? She deserves better than some guy who is staring at her sister all the time."

Caro sighed, hiding behind her wine glass as she snuck another glance in Finn's direction.

"Look, I've considered it...but you know Cait isn't exactly my biggest fan. She'll think I'm trying to sabotage her, or get attention, or both. She already thinks I'm a narcissist. Imagine if I walked over to her and told her that her boyfriend is making eyes at anything that moves, including me. I can just hear her now in that shrill little voice. '*You always make everything about you, Caro! Why are you so self-obsessed*'?" Caro squawked. Olivia was taken by surprise, choking on her wine as she laughed. Caitlin's eyes swiveled to them and she glared at them as they giggled. Olivia knew she hadn't heard what they were talking about, but she did feel a little guilty. Caro snickered, nudging Olivia with her elbow.

"See what I mean? She's always prepared to see the worst in me. I can't do anything right. But hey…maybe you could talk to her this weekend? I think she'd listen to you, if you're subtle."

"I don't know…she's seen me hanging out with you. Maybe she'll think you put me up to it."

"Well, I did." Caro sighed. "This is why I just don't bother anymore. She's got eyes of her own. She's a smart girl, smarter than me. If she's not seeing this side of Finn, it's because she's choosing not to. She needs to realize she can do better on her own."

Olivia knew Caro was right, but she still felt bad. Finn had finally torn his eyes away from Caro for a while, but the effect of his gaze remained. Olivia wondered if he had driven Caro and Caitlin even further apart, or whether they'd always been so hostile with each other. Olivia knew sibling rivalry to an extent —she often competed with Veronica back when they were kids. But the level of bitterness between her cousins made her feel sad. Didn't they know they were lucky to have one another?

The night got hazier as they went on. Olivia got swept up in it all, making the rounds. She went over to play with the young kids in the other room. She made small talk with Uncle Mark in the kitchen, laughing at all his loud jokes. She and Caro roped Jean into taking a tequila shot, then collapsed in a fit of giggles as Olivia's mother coughed and pursed her lips roughly.

Then she sat on the sofa with Caitlin and Finn for a while, catching up. She wasn't sure if she imagined a coldness in Caitlin toward her, but she was glad that Finn kept to himself, choosing to stare across the room at Caro instead. When he got up to go to the bathroom, Olivia almost told Caitlin what was on her mind, but she bit her tongue. *Don't get involved, don't get involved…* it was becoming her mantra for the weekend.

As the evening drew on and the moon's reflection began to shine on the lake, Uncle Mark insisted that they take their drinks outside to enjoy the air. Olivia found herself at Caro's side once again, drawn to her energy. They sat in comfortable silence on deckchairs for a while as Caro texted, sipping from her wine glass. After a while, Uncle Mark appeared and snatched the phone from her grasp.

"Hey, come on!" Caro whined like a kid. She was a little tipsy and her words slurred. Uncle Mark shook his head.

"This is family time, Caro. You don't need to be texting right now."

"Alright, alright! I'll just make a call later, no biggie. Can I have the phone back?"

Uncle Mark rolled his eyes before handing Caro's phone back to her. She slid it into her pocket, but Olivia caught Stephanie and Caitlin looking over judgmentally. Olivia would've felt sorry for Caro, except she knew she didn't care at all. She smiled lazily at Olivia, raising her eyebrows.

"It's like a prison here. He confiscated my vape, too. I feel like a kid again," Caro said. She grabbed Olivia's hand. "But it's not all bad. I'm back with my favorite cousin."

"Favorite, huh? That's quite the statement."

"Well, it's true. You've always been my favorite. Is that terrible to say, given what happened with Veronica?"

Hearing her sister's name was like a knife in the back for Olivia, but she kept her face straight. It was a familiar enough sensation now that she knew how to hide her true feelings. She knew Caro meant no harm anyway. She shrugged, looking out to the water.

"You and I were always closest. Veronica did her own thing."

"Yes, exactly, that's what I meant. She used to be closer with Cody and Caitlin. Mostly Cait, really. Which was strange because I don't think they had all that much in common. But it worked for us, didn't it?" She glanced over at her sister with a frown. "Look at her now. Sitting with the wicked stepmother instead of with her cousin. She's such a suckup. Okay, no, I shouldn't say that, it's cruel. But it's kind of true. I feel bad. I actually do."

Olivia looked over, remembering how Caitlin and Veronica would always go off together, leaving her with Caro. Even though she'd come to terms with the absence of her sister, it still felt like such a gaping hole in the family.

"It was better back then. She'd have Veronica, I'd have you. Then she and I wouldn't bicker and we could actually have fun.

Now it's all different, isn't it?" Caro asked, an uncharacteristically reflective tone in her voice.

"At least she's got Finn with her…"

"Yeah, I guess, but he's hardly good company when he's ogling other women, is he? He's fine, I suppose. But I think she must be feeling her absence today."

Olivia sighed. "Yeah. Me too, to be honest."

Caro laid her cheek against Olivia's shoulder gently. Olivia could smell the wine on her breath. She wondered how many glasses they'd drunk between them.

"You're so strong, Olivia," Caro whispered. "I wouldn't know what to do with myself, if…"

She trailed off and cast a look at her sister. The two crossed eyes for only a moment, but Caitlin rolled her eyes and Caro responded in kind. The moment of sincerity was gone, shoved right back underneath the feud they'd been carrying on their entire lives.

"Nobody does," Olivia said, her throat tight. "But that's why we appreciate the time we've got."

"How do you do it?" Caro asked. "It's like you're made of stronger stuff. You're so put together."

Olivia laughed bitterly. "I'm really not."

Caro frowned, holding on tight to her. "You are. You really are. Don't doubt yourself, cousin. You're a real one."

Olivia offered her a playful smile. "So five-drink-Caro is kind of emotional, huh?"

Caro was a little slow to respond, but then she laughed loudly. "I guess so. Maybe I need to walk it off a little. Hey, you won't tell if I sneak off for a bit to make a call, will you?"

"Course not. To be honest, I might turn in. All those hot dogs made me sleepy."

"Alright, well I'll see you in the morning then, yeah? Or maybe like early afternoon. I don't really do mornings…"

She squeezed Olivia's shoulder as she slipped away. No one else seemed to notice, all of them caught up in an alcoholic daze. Olivia caught Brock's eye across the yard and he nodded back toward the house, sensing Olivia's need to get away from it all.

She nodded and they walked back up to the lake house, meeting in the middle to wrap their arms around one another.

"You okay?" Brock asked, planting a kiss on top of her head. Olivia nodded.

"Yeah…I'm good. Today has been good."

"And tomorrow will be too. Unless we're hungover. Then it'll be awful."

"Better chug some water before bed then. Caro has been drinking me under the table."

Olivia crawled into bed with a happy buzz beneath her skin. Looking out over the lake, she could just about see Caro in the distance, walking toward the trees with her phone pressed to her ear. She closed her eyes, glad to reconnect, glad to let loose, glad to relax.

She slept better than she had in weeks.

# CHAPTER EIGHT

OLIVIA WOKE UP FEELING A LITTLE GROGGY. SHE HADN'T slept so well in a while, and it was almost like her body didn't appreciate being well rested. It had forgotten how it felt to get a decent night's sleep. But there was sunlight streaming in from the cracks in the curtains, and Olivia smiled, warmth filling her chest. *Today's going to be a good day,* she told herself.

Brock stirred beside her and Olivia cuddled in close, closing her eyes to savor her moment alone with him. It wasn't often they were undisturbed by work or tragedy; it felt good to just ease into his touch for a while. His arms wrapped around her and he kissed the top of her head gently, his eyes barely open yet.

"Morning," he said, his voice scratchy and deep. Olivia loved that when he'd been drinking, his voice was always like this the next day. It was sexy and funny. "Did you sleep well?"

"Better than in a long while."

"Good. I knew this weekend would be good for you." He held her tighter. "You deserve a break."

Olivia smiled sadly. It was nearly impossible to take a break from grief, but she did feel a little better. She hadn't expected her family vacation to feel so wholesome after so many years, but she was glad of the distraction, and despite the tensions within the group, she was glad to see all of them. The last of the Knights would bee due to arrive that morning, and then they'd all be together again. One big happy family, if that was something that was still possible. She didn't realize it was something she wanted until she had been a part of it all the night before. It felt like home, even after so long of being apart from all of them. That was the thing about family, she thought. They're always there.

"I think I smell bacon," Brock said with a hopeful sniff in the air. Olivia rolled her eyes with a smile.

"Alright, let's go and investigate."

The pair of them dressed and headed down to the kitchen. Olivia suspected it would be her Uncle Mark in the kitchen, and she was right. Stephanie was lounging on the sofa with cucumber slices placed over her eyes and a facemask smothered over her face. Gentle music was playing in the background, like they were on a spa retreat. Uncle Mark caught sight of Olivia and gave her a wry smile, putting a finger to his lips.

"She doesn't like to be disturbed when she's doing her treatments," he whispered as she stepped into the kitchen. "Though I think she's got about five minutes before this whole place descends into hell again. The smell of food will draw everyone out. It always does."

Olivia marveled at the massive spread before her. In addition to the bacon, hash browns, eggs, and sausages Mark was currently tending to on the stove, there was a massive plate of cut-up fruit, a bowl of waffle batter set out right next to the waffle maker along with butter and syrup, cinnamon rolls fresh out of the oven, and

ELLE GRAY | K.S. GRAY

even a box of donuts from the donut shop in town. It looked incredible and smelled even better.

"Brock smelled that bacon from a mile off. Can I help with breakfast at all?"

"Absolutely not. You just relax and put your feet up. The table is all set and there's juice on the counter if you want some? Or coffee?"

"Coffee," Olivia said sleepily, crossing the room to use the machine. "I keep getting hit with a wave of nostalgia. You always did these big breakfasts back in the day."

He chuckled deeply. "I sure did. And there was never a scrap left over afterwards! I guess I kind of wanted to recreate the old days. It's been a difficult few years for the family, hasn't it? Especially for you and your mother."

Olivia nodded. A lot had happened in the ten years since they had last all met up at the lake house, including her uncle's divorce and remarriage to Stephanie. But somehow, that had hardly registered for Olivia when she had been too busy grieving her sister's death and her mother's disappearance. It had never occurred to Olivia that while she was losing a sister, everyone else was losing a cousin, a niece, a friend. It was selfish of her to be so self-centered, she knew, but it was also rational. It just wasn't the same for them as it was for her.

"You and your mom have been very strong. I wish that I had reached out more," Uncle Mark told Olivia, clearly caught up in his own guilty conscience. "But your mom is very... independent."

Olivia chuckled. "That's one way of putting it."

Mark nodded. "I never wanted to get in her way, or make her feel suffocated, you know? And then when she went missing... well, you're your mother's daughter. I thought you'd want the space too."

Olivia fidgeted uncomfortably, waiting for the coffee machine to do its thing. Would she have accepted her uncle's support back then? Maybe not. He was right—she was very much like her mother, wearing her heart on her sleeve but pushing away help when it was offered to her. But would she have appreciated hearing from him at the lowest point in her life? Absolutely. She had been going through the loneliest period of her life and she didn't hear a peep from anyone. She just had to grit her teeth and get on with it, praying for solutions that never came.

It was making her nostalgia turn sour. It had been a nice idea to return to the way things were ten years ago, but they couldn't stay in the past. Because in their present, everything was broken.

"It's in the past," Olivia said, though she wasn't convincing herself, let alone anyone else. Her uncle smiled, but she could tell he was uncomfortable, likely wishing he hadn't said anything at all.

He cleared his throat and returned his attention to the stove. "It's been good to see you. And we just adore you. It's nice to have everyone back under one roof."

Olivia nodded, collecting her coffee from beneath the machine. She found she didn't have much left to say to her uncle, harsh as it sounded. It was making her feel angry and disappointed to know that he had waited all this time to reach out to her and her mom, to make an effort after everything they'd been through. It was like he had waited for the dust to settle, for their aching hearts to mend a little so he wouldn't have to deal with the difficult feelings and the agony of it all. Olivia had been second guessing herself a moment ago, wondering if it had been her job to check in on everyone when Veronica passed away, but it was a two-way street, and no one had crossed it for her. Perhaps this was why her mom didn't make much effort to keep up with the family. She had never said it aloud, but it made sense now. If her own brother didn't take care of her, then who would?

Olivia was glad to hear the sound of footsteps on the stairs, likely one of her cousins getting up out of bed. She pushed her issue with her uncle aside, telling herself that she would have to get over it until it was time to leave. Just a couple of days and then she would be able to leave this all behind. She was disappointed that her bubble had burst, but she was wary of them all now, and it made her feel tired and lonely. *Not long now. Just get through this,* she told herself.

Caitlin entered the kitchen, shortly followed by Finn behind her. Finn nodded to Olivia, but it was clear his eyes were scanning the room for signs of Caro. Olivia wrinkled her nose. Caitlin had terrible taste in men.

"Morning," Caitlin said, planting a kiss on her father's cheek. "It smells good in here."

"Well, it's nearly ready. Do me a favor and go poke your sister. Otherwise she'll miss breakfast."

"Shame," Caitlin said coldly, taking a seat at the table to make her position on the matter known. Finn hovered by the door, practically bouncing on the balls of his feet.

"I could go—"

"Sit down," Caitlin snapped. The room turned cold at the sound of her voice. Olivia swallowed back her discomfort. At least Caitlin seemed to have more of a backbone than she once had. Was she starting to notice the vibe that Finn adopted whenever Caro was around? Was she starting to see that he wasn't a good boyfriend to her?

Olivia sat down opposite Caitlin at the table and Brock appeared from the living room, sliding into the chair beside her. The room began to fill with chatter and guests. Hannah and Heather entered with their kids, Stephanie showed up, her facemask washed away, and then Jean arrived, looking fresh-faced and smiling. At least she was enjoying herself, Olivia thought. She was glad that her mother's weekend wouldn't be tainted by the bitter feeling she had in her own heart. She didn't want to ruin this for her mother, even if her conversation with her uncle had ruined it for her.

"Order up!" Uncle Mark declared as he began to place platters of food in the middle of the table. Olivia let the smell of sausages and eggs and bacon fill her nose as people began to pile their plates high. She made small talk with Caitlin and the little cousins Erik and Brayden as she ate, forgetting for a while that anything had upset her.

Halfway through the breakfast, two more guests arrived—Cody wheeled his grandmother, Tina, in just as Brock was about to have a second round of food and Olivia had to slap his hand away from the plates to make sure there was some left. Cody had filled out since Olivia last saw him, becoming tall and muscular, but he still had a shy manner about him, and he waved to her awkwardly across the table before helping his grandmother with her breakfast. The room was filled with noise and energy, but the table was missing one person.

"Where on earth is Caroline?" Grandma Tina asked, chewing on a piece of bacon that she had picked up with her leathery fingers. "Girl barely eats as it is. Did you not call her to come downstairs?"

"Leave her be," Stephanie said with a sniff. "If she wants to be rude, let her. It's nothing new. Barely emerges before noon if she can get away with it."

Olivia glanced at her uncle, half expecting him to defend his daughter, but she was disappointed to see that he stayed silent, focusing on his plate and refusing to look up. Olivia bit the inside of her cheek. *Coward,* she thought. Her opinion of him was getting worse by the minute. What kind of father didn't stand up for his daughter? The tension between the family hadn't exactly escaped her notice, but Olivia thought it was cruel to leave Stephanie's comments hanging in the air, especially when Caro wasn't around to defend herself.

But Olivia had to admit that once the subject passed, the mood was much better. If Caro was the one causing all of the issues in the family, then maybe it made sense that things ran smoother while she wasn't there. Was she hiding up in her room deliberately, hoping to avoid the drama? Was this what she had grown accustomed to? The thought made Olivia feel sad. Did her family really think so little of her that they preferred it when she wasn't around? Judging by Caitlin's coldness, by Stephanie's cruelty, and Mark's indifference, Olivia could guess that was the case.

There wasn't a scrap of food left by the time the family finished eating. There was none left for Caro if she did decide to make an appearance. Caitlin helped clear the table, ever the doting daughter, and Olivia found herself wishing that Caro would come downstairs and join them, if only to cause a little mischief again. She appreciated that about her cousin. She did as she pleased, even though the family disapproved. It was an inspiration, honestly. But she still hadn't appeared when Stephanie announced that they would be going on a walk alongside the lake and through the forest.

"It's a family tradition," she declared, though she hadn't even been a part of the family the last time they'd all been there together. Olivia caught her mother's eye as they shrugged on their jackets and the pair of them smirked a little. They had made this walk many times before. Olivia used to follow the same path down to the woods to play among the trees with Caro and Caitlin, rain or shine. Veronica complained, without fail, that she was getting cold every single time they ventured out. The thought made her smile, even in her absence now.

They all set off as a pack into the brisk morning, Cody leading the way with Grandma Tina and the rest of them keeping pace behind them. It was a very slow walk, the kind that made Olivia's legs ache from the effort of moving slower than usual, but she shuffled along quietly, sticking close to Brock and her mother. She wasn't in the mood to try small talking with the children again, and the thought of hearing Stephanie or Caitlin complain more about her wasn't appealing. Olivia thought she ought to make a little effort with Cody, but for the moment, she had no desire to talk to any of them at all. They were a strange bunch, her family, and she didn't feel the same happiness to be there that she had the night before. Perhaps it was the lack of wine, or the lack of Caro's sunny presence. Whichever it was, she hoped that one or the other would show up again soon.

The lake was beautiful, at least, the water shimmering in the mid-morning sunlight. They headed toward the forest and Olivia recalled doing the walk as a child, looking up at the tall trees and being scared of them. They didn't scare her now—given that she lived in a forest, she had gotten used to them—but as they headed into the trees, she was surprised a little by the sudden darkness that swallowed them up, the leaves blocking out most of the light. With the absence of light came a cold shudder on Olivia's spine. It was certainly cooler in the forest, but the quietness of their group and the shadowy trees made the whole thing feel a little creepy.

And then there was a cry that seemed to ricochet through the entire forest. It was coming from Grandma Tina up ahead of the group. Instinctively, Olivia rushed forward, driven to help her. But when she saw the reason that Tina had cried out, she stopped dead in her tracks, her stomach dropping.

Lying on the forest floor, slightly obscured by a tree and completely motionless, was Caro.

# CHAPTER NINE

"**S**TAY BACK, EVERYBODY STAY BACK," BROCK SAID, rushing to Caro's side. Olivia watched him in horror, clocking the moment he gasped and took a step back from where she lay. He turned back to the family, his expression grave. "She's taken quite a hit to the back of her head...I don't think..."

"Check her pulse!" Uncle Mark cried. "Oh God, Caro..."

Brock wavered and Olivia could see from the look in his eyes that he knew there was no point. But he kneeled beside her and gently took her limp wrist in his hand. He felt her pressure point for ten long seconds, everyone holding their breath.

Olivia had seen enough bodies to know when a person was dead. Caro's skin was ghostly white, her eyes glassy and unblinking.

There was no denying that she was gone, and yet Olivia hoped for a miracle. Brock swallowed and shook his head.

"I'm sorry... she's gone. She's cold... I think she has been for a while."

Olivia clapped a hand over her mouth to stop herself from crying out in horror. How did this happen? She recalled Caro's retreating figure heading into the forest the night before on her phone. Had she been out here all this time? She must have been. While they had been feasting and enjoying a hearty breakfast, she'd been lying dead in the woods. If only they had checked her bedroom earlier. If only they had checked in, then this might not have happened...

But Olivia knew that wasn't true. Caro hadn't simply died by accident. Something had hit her hard enough on the back of her head to kill her. That was no accident.

Somebody had wanted to hurt her.

To kill her.

Olivia could hear her family falling apart all around her, but they were muffled by her own emotions. She stumbled forward, needing to see her, needing to make sure this was real. Brock tried to stop her but she shook her head. "I need to see it, Brock."

She moved around the side of the tree to see her cousin's body in full view. She was trembling as she saw the back of Caro's head caved in with dark, dried blood puddled on the forest floor. Now she understood why Brock hadn't felt the need to feel for her pulse. There was no surviving a blow like that. Olivia swallowed as she sank to her knees and slid her hand in Caro's cold one. She had died out here all alone, probably terrified, while the whole family had slept soundly in their beds. But why? Who would want to hurt her?

Olivia turned to look back at her grieving family. The children were crying now as the twins tried to usher them away back to the house. Caitlin's face was plastered with shock, but no tears fell from her eyes. Stephanie was tight lipped, looking more confused than hurt. Cody was sobbing, gripping Grandma Tina's hand, and Mark looked completely lost, his eyes vacant. Surely none of them would want this? Surely, despite all the tension, none of them would want to kill Caro?

But now, the thought wouldn't leave Olivia alone. What if one of them had done this? Not one of them loved Caro unconditionally. She was a thorn in their side, the difficult one in the family. But had those petty squabbles been enough for one of them to kill?

"Olivia."

Olivia turned to the sound of Brock's voice. He gave her a knowing look. A look that told her to stop spiraling, to focus. He knew her well enough to know that her mind had already begun trying to untangle the mess they were in, to solve the case instead of focusing on the hurt she held inside her. Olivia could feel tears falling silently down her cheeks, but he was right. They couldn't just stay there. They needed to call the police. They needed to try and figure out what had happened to Caro, before it was too late to tell. Olivia swallowed and took her hand away from Caro's.

"Can you make the call?" Olivia asked Brock. He was the most detached from the situation, and the one best equipped to deal with it. He nodded.

"I'll do it. Will you be okay?"

Olivia nodded, though her heart ached so hard it felt like it might cease to function. It was still healing from Jonathan's death, and now she had another loss to deal with. But she didn't have time to acknowledge her pain. She wanted justice for Caro. Beautiful, wild Caro, the girl who had it all until she had nothing. Her life had been snatched from her so fast. Seeing her now, eyes open, jaw slack, skull broken, Olivia could hardly believe she had been alive only twelve hours before, bringing life to the party, making her laugh through all of her own pain. There had been so much life inside her that it seemed impossible that she could ever die, the kind of soul who was immortal even after she was gone. Why would anyone want to do this to her? Who was capable?

Olivia didn't have the answers, but she knew one thing for sure.

For now, she didn't trust a single person.

The police arrived within the hour, taping off the area where Caro had died. Jean had insisted that the family return to the house, leaving Brock and Olivia at the scene to speak to the police. Brock was in the process of relaying the situation to one of the officers while Olivia tried her hardest to hold herself together. It was easier to let him do the talking while she absorbed all she could from the scene.

"No one had seen her since last night," Brock said. "Olivia and I headed to bed just before midnight, and we saw Caroline walking toward the trees. She was making a phone call to somebody, though I'm not sure who. The party died down shortly afterward and everybody headed to bed, but no one saw Caroline return."

"Nobody saw her this morning?" asked the sheriff, a no-nonsense veteran who had introduced herself as Angie McCarty.

Brock shook his head. "She tends to sleep in late. It wasn't so suspicious when she didn't come down for breakfast. She also drank a fair amount last night...I guess we all thought that she was sleeping it off."

"I see."

The sheriff jotted it down in her notes.

"Olivia and I did a preliminary sweep of the scene and we didn't find any murder weapon. But in my opinion, it was almost certainly an attack. There are no rocks nearby, nothing that could have been an accident. It's not like she tripped and fell on a rock. This was a targeted attack."

McCarty looked up and frowned. "I'm sorry, and you are?"

Brock showed his badge, but it was a slow, resigned motion, not the usual confident, cool way he flipped it. "Special Agent Brock Tanner. Olivia and I work for the FBI, we deal with deaths like this often...but it's still no less shocking to see."

Olivia closed her eyes, removing herself from the moment for a while. It was more than she could cope with. Hearing them speak about her cousin in such a way felt wrong, and it took her back to her sister's death. This weekend had forced her to think about Veronica far too many times already. And now this. Once again, the Grim Reaper was trailing her, leaving a path of destruction and pain wherever she went.

Her throat felt raw as she opened her eyes again. She didn't want to step aside and let someone else handle this. Pained as she was, she wanted to help, to make sure that Caro's death was avenged. She deserved that at least. And if nothing else, the family would get closure on what had happened. Olivia would see to it.

That was, if the family weren't responsible.

It was a harrowing thought to imagine that anyone in her family was cold-blooded enough to strike Caro down. And for what? To solve petty family squabbles? To resolve a case of jealousy, or irritation, or something equally as irrelevant? Her thoughts raced, counting off each person in the lake house. Caitlin, the jealous sister. Finn, the creepy boyfriend. Stephanie, barely a step down from an evil stepmother. Mark, the apathetic father. The cousins, uncles, nieces, aunts, cousins, too many to consider. If one of them did it, she would figure them out.

But if it wasn't one of them, then who else could it be?

Olivia had thought they were safe out there. They were secluded, away from the rest of the world. This was supposed to be an escape for the weekend, a chance to reboot after such a series of unfortunate events in her life. Now, it was becoming another nightmare for her to face up to.

She took a steadying breath, casting another glance toward Caro's body. The blow to the back of her head had been hard. Whoever had done it had to have some strength in their body, and plenty of violence locked inside them. Did that rule anyone out? She wasn't sure. But it did solidify one thing in Olivia's mind—this was a crime of passion. It was possible it was someone Caro didn't know, but it didn't seem likely. To kill someone with such force, there was usually a reason.

Her mind whirled with possibilities. Love and hate were the two most passionate emotions on the planet, and so often the cause of so much tragedy. Caro didn't know much love from her own family, but Olivia wasn't sure she was hated, either. So who else could be a suspect? A scorned former lover? A friend who had been rejected? An obsessive stalker? Somehow, she could picture any one of those things being applicable. Caro was pretty, and friendly, and flirtatious, and had always had a fling or two going on. Had someone taken things too far?

"May I?" Olivia asked the police officer quietly, gesturing beyond the yellow tape as she returned to reality. After a moment of hesitation, the woman nodded and then returned to interviewing Brock. Olivia slowly moved toward the bands of yellow tape, ducking underneath and steeling herself to face Caro's body again.

She knelt down beside her, examining her body with gentle care. She was glad that Caro was face down so that she didn't need to see her face while she examined the back of her head. Her hair was matted with blood, and there was a visible dent in her head, like a deep thumb print in a wad of clay. Olivia was sure that it would be determined that she died on impact. One brutal, hard swing to the back of the head had killed her, throwing her to the ground with force. She would have been dead before she hit the ground. Despite the bloody mess of it all, it calmed Olivia a little to know that her cousin hadn't suffered.

There didn't seem to be any other indicators on her body as to what had happened. No bruising anywhere except her nose, given that she had fallen face first on the ground. It didn't look as though someone had grabbed her or tried to hurt her first. But whoever had met her in the forest had obviously come prepared for an altercation, given that they'd found something hard enough to kill her with one blow to the head. Olivia scanned the area for anything that might have been used as a weapon, but as Brock had informed the officer, they'd already been unsuccessful in their first attempt, and she didn't know why she thought the answer might magically pop up in front of her this time.

She stayed beside her cousin a little longer. She felt scared to stand up, to leave her there alone again. It was too horrific to picture her final moments, to see her life taken away from her in her mind's eye. Olivia closed her eyes again, trying to block out those images. But they stayed with her even after she returned to Brock's side, trying to stop her hands from trembling.

Brock had finished his statement and they turned to watch the police working. Brock's hand found the small of Olivia's back, offering her a small amount of comfort. He took a deep breath, preparing himself for something he was about to say. It put Olivia on edge.

"There's something you should know," Brock said calmly, though his face was worried. Olivia folded her arms around herself, frowning.

"What is it?"

"I woke up in the night to get a glass of water. I headed downstairs and everything was quiet. I assumed everyone was in bed. But as I was about to go back upstairs, I saw your cousin coming back inside. She was kicking off her shoes, taking off her coat..."

"Caro?" Olivia asked sharply, her heart skipping a beat. Brock shook his head.

"No, it was Caitlin. I don't think Caro ever made it back to the house. But this was late...probably around two. She didn't acknowledge me, so I guess she didn't think anyone was awake. And then a moment later, Finn came inside too."

"So they were out there together? At two in the morning? What on earth for?"

Brock shook his head. "Who knows...it could be innocent. Maybe they were having an argument...things seemed frosty between them this morning. I suppose they took it away from the house to make sure they weren't overheard by anyone. It would explain a lot. But we also have to consider that they could have been out there at the time of Caro's death. I mean, I don't imagine that Caro was on that call for two whole hours...if she had been able to, I think she would've come back to the house no later than like, twelve-thirty, right? Plenty of time for her to wrap up her conversation and then come back. Why would she choose to be out there alone for any longer than she had to be? But I think she was dead by then. And everyone else was in bed."

"Except Caitlin and Finn," Olivia finished. Brock nodded.

"I'm not about to start pointing fingers. You know how risky that can be. But I thought it was important that you had all of the information. I know that Caitlin is your family, and that Caro was her sister… but we're out in the middle of nowhere. In theory, we are the only ones who knew Caro would be out here. And I don't know their relationship, but if it's anything like what I saw yesterday, it was…"

"Cold at the best of times," Olivia finished. "But not enough to murder her, surely?"

She genuinely didn't know. It had been so long since she'd spent time with the family that she couldn't see Caitlin killing her own sister in cold blood. But some part of her wondered…

Brock sighed. "I'm not saying she did it. All I'm saying is…"

"Is that we can't rule anything out," Olivia said. "I agree. She's not the only one with motive, though. I think there's something strange going on in my family… and I need to dig up whatever it is if we're going to get answers about what happened to Caro."

"Are you sure this is something you can handle? After everything that we've been through lately…I don't want you to push yourself too far. Especially when we're going to have to investigate your own family."

Olivia thought back to how she had felt that morning, when it became clear that her family had turned her back on her in her greatest hour of need. They hadn't been there to see her through her sister's death, or the disappearance of her mother, or any of the traumatic things she'd endured in recent years. But to turn her back on them now would be like turning her back on Caro, and that wasn't something she was willing to do. No matter her past with her family, she had to step up now and fix this.

Even if it meant finding a killer amongst them.

"I can do this," Olivia insisted. "I have to. For Caro."

# CHAPTER TEN

O LIVIA AND BROCK RETURNED TO THE LAKE HOUSE alongside Sheriff McCarty. She seemed capable of leading the way to Olivia, and she wondered if she should leave the investigation in her hands. But every time she thought about her beautiful cousin lying dead in the dirt, she knew she wouldn't be able to leave this alone. She had the expertise to offer, even if the police had it covered. Murder investigations weren't common in small towns such as this. She would be able to give them help wherever they might need it. Maybe then she could push aside the guilt she felt. She shouldn't have let Caro walk off into the forest alone. She should have kept an eye out for her coming back.

And now because she hadn't, Caro was dead.

Back in the house, everyone was distraught. Mark had his head in his hands, Stephanie's hands placed firmly on his shoulders to calm him down. Caitlin was staring into space while Jared quietly comforted her. Hannah, Heather, and Jean tried desperately to distract the kids, but their hearts weren't in it. Finn was standing separately from Caitlin, saying nothing and keeping his eyes trained on the ground. Roger seemed to have withdrawn back to his sullen self on the recliner. Cody had fetched his inhaler and was trying his best to keep breathing while Grandma Tina dabbed her eyes beside him. Olivia's eyes scanned over them all and she wondered which of them knew more than they were letting on. Which of them could she truly trust? She hated the idea that she couldn't trust her family, but it was her job—and her nature—to be suspicious. Her eyes fell on Caitlin. Did she have anything to say for herself? Did she even care about what had happened?

It didn't seem like it, from her dry eyes and solemn, but unemotional expression. It was like she was simply in a bad mood, or her team had just lost in a game. She didn't look like someone who had lost her only sister. But Olivia tried not to let too many wild speculations fly in her head. Everyone grieves differently.

"Let me start by saying I'm truly sorry for your loss," McCarty said, addressing the room. "We're going to need to know exactly where you all were and when last night. This will help us paint a picture of what happened to Caroline."

"We were all in bed, of course," Stephanie snapped. "*She* was the one who chose to go off gallivanting on her own, always causing problems."

"Actually, Mr. Tanner's testimony says otherwise," McCarty said, turning to him. "He recalls coming downstairs around two in the morning and seeing two of you returning from somewhere. Which one of you is Caitlin?"

Caitlin's eyes widened at the mention of her name. Over the initial shock, she glared at Brock. Olivia narrowed her eyes at her. Why was she acting so shifty? Did she have something to hide after all?

"Finn and I stepped out briefly last night," she said tersely. "We took a walk around the lake."

"At what time?"

"Just after midnight."

"And you were out for around two hours, then?"

"I guess so," Caitlin said tightly. Olivia never took her eyes off her cousin. She was acting oddly and it wasn't helping with Olivia's suspicions that someone in the family had wanted to hurt Caro. The sisters had been at odds their entire lives. Had Caitlin finally snapped and taken matters into her own hands?

"You didn't go into the forest at all, then?" McCarty asked. Her questioning wasn't accusatory, but Caitlin's nostrils flared.

"Of course not."

"Just a question, ma'am. So you avoided the woods, and you didn't hear or see anything suspicious? It's likely that your sister died at some point during your walk. If she made any noise at all, it might have been heard from the lake. Perhaps you forgot about some details that might be relevant now?"

"I haven't forgotten anything," Caitlin said angrily. Her arms were folded over her chest. "Finn and I were having a discussion, not that it's anyone's business. That's the honest truth. I wasn't thinking about anything else, least of all my sister."

"The honest truth is the only kind of truth," McCarty pointed out. "You seem very defensive of these questions."

"Because funny enough, my life doesn't revolve around Caro. Though I'm sure she thought it did. I wasn't thinking about anything else except for my conversation with Finn. Least of all my sister."

Olivia felt a rush of anger to her surviving cousin. Was she really holding on to bitterness after what they'd seen in the forest? Caitlin must've felt Olivia staring because her gaze locked onto hers and held it for a moment, defiant. It made Olivia want to shudder. There was a coldness to Caitlin that she had never known before. When had she switched off so completely? She had always imagined the rivalry between her and Caro was just a sibling thing, not so serious as to remain in such an awful situation. But from the look in Caitlin's eyes, she didn't care at all that Caro was gone.

In fact, perhaps she was glad.

"Well, if anything comes to mind, you'll need to let us know. Anything small might tell us more about what happened to your sister. As you can imagine, every piece of information is crucial."

"Understood," Caitlin said curtly. "But like I said. I haven't forgotten anything."

McCarty glanced at Olivia, looking a little lost. Olivia had dealt with her fair share of difficult interviews in her time, but she never expected her family members to be so standoffish with a police officer, especially given that she was only trying to help. McCarty cleared her throat.

"Was anybody else awake after midnight?"

Hannah was the first to speak up. "Heather, Jared, and I are staying at the hotel down the road. We left with the kids at around ten last night and didn't come back 'til this morning."

"Grandma Tina and I only arrived this morning," Cody wheezed, still focusing on his breathing. "I haven't seen or spoken to Caro in a few months."

"Was that unusual for you?"

"Not really," he shrugged. "We got along I guess, but we're not super close. She tends to go off the grid a lot of the time."

"So you wouldn't be able to tell me if anything felt off about her lately?"

Cody shook his head. "No. Like I said, we haven't really been in contact. I was looking forward to seeing her." He glanced over at Caitlin, who rolled her eyes viciously, dismissing his search for approval. "I don't think I've really spoken to her in at least a year."

"A *year?*" Olivia sputtered. She couldn't keep the shock out of her voice. Had none of them really been in contact with her for a full year? But even as she said it, she knew it wasn't impossible. She herself had had her struggles in the last year and beyond. But even she texted her cousins regularly at least every few weeks. How disconnected had they become?

"Maybe not quite that long… we texted a couple times. But I don't even remember the last time I saw her. She didn't come home for Christmas…"

*I wonder why,* Olivia thought, wishing she could say it aloud. After the way things had shaken out, she couldn't picture Caro being made to feel welcome at any important gathering, let alone Christmas. She had an image of her cousin sitting all alone in a dark apartment, guzzling wine and poking at a sad microwave meal during the holidays. The thought was so depressing it brought a tear to her eye.

"She didn't want anything to do with us," Stephanie butted in. "She thought she was too good for us all of a sudden."

Cody turned red, clearing his throat. "I don't think..."

"It wasn't all of a sudden. She's always been that way," Caitlin sneered. "We got sick of chasing her around, so she stopped coming around."

Mark held up his hands. "Can we all just calm down?" he said loudly, trying to tamp down things before they exploded. "She's *gone,* Caitlin. Have some respect."

Caitlin turned to her father with unshed tears bristling in her eyes. "Like she did for us? Sure, I'll have some *respect.* I'll just keep my mouth shut. I don't have anything good to say anyway."

"Do not speak about your sister that way—"

"Can't we just try to figure out who—"

"She was always such a b—"

"What is this, the Caroline hate society?"

"I can't believe you would say that—"

"Oh, like *you're* one to talk!"

"Please, everyone, the children..."

Olivia's heart sank as the room instantly fell into chaos. They bickered and fought and yelled and went straight for the jugular. It wasn't just limited to Caroline, either; old wounds were reopened and accusations were flung to every corner of the room. The children began wailing, only outmatched by the shouts and screams of Caitlin and Stephanie tearing each other to pieces.

"Enough! That's enough!" Sheriff McCarty yelled, but even her imposing demeanor wasn't enough to quiet everyone down. They were Knights, after all, and when they got their teeth into something, they would never let it go without a fight. Olivia knew that all too well.

"She said that's *enough!*" Brock roared, his deep voice echoing in the room so loud it nearly hurt Olivia's ears. But it did the trick. The room fell silent and everyone looked ashamed. Olivia found herself seething. She'd never expected such hate from her family members, and it wounded her so deeply to hear them being so cruel when Caro wasn't even in the ground yet. What had caused such a rift between them all?

"Thank you, Mr. Tanner," Sheriff McCarty said quietly. She directed a piercing glare to everyone in the room. "Any more outbursts like that and I'll personally escort each and every one of you downtown. Do I make myself clear?"

Everyone nodded sullenly, still avoiding her glare.

"Now that that's settled… has anyone else got anything to say about last night? I need confirmation from everyone I haven't heard from yet."

"I woke briefly in the night, but I didn't see or hear anything. Roger and I stayed in the bedroom," Jean told McCarty. The others began to murmur similar alibis and Olivia watched each of them in turn, looking for telltale signs of lies, but she saw none. Stephanie seemed a little uncomfortable under Olivia's gaze, but that didn't surprise her. Given how Stephanie had treated her step-daughter, it was clear she had no love for the girl. Stephanie was likely feeling under scrutiny, her more recent addition to the family a point of suspicion. Especially from her FBI agent relatives.

"Thank you for cooperating," McCarty said once everyone had made their statements. "I have a few other things to discuss. We found Caroline's phone on her person. Given that she was last seen making a phone call, we'd like to access her mobile as soon as possible. Does anyone happen to know the passcode to enter her phone? It would help immensely if we can get into her records sooner rather than later."

"I recommend trying her birthday. Ten, zero eight, nine two. She always was a narcissist," Caitlin said bitterly.

"That's enough, Cait," Mark murmured, but he barely raised his voice. McCarty quietly tapped the numbers into the phone.

"No. That's not it," she said. Olivia chewed her lip, trying to think of something significant enough for Caro to use it. A memory passed through her mind.

"Try thirteen, thirteen, thirteen," Olivia said quietly. Everyone stared at her like she was crazy. Olivia's eyes fell to the ground.

"She always used to say, '*thirteen... unlucky for some, but not for me*.' She used to get me to call her Lady Luck," Olivia murmured. McCarty wavered before inputting the number. She swallowed as the screen changed.

"That's the code," McCarty confirmed. Olivia nodded, unsurprised. How was it that she understood Caro better than her closest family? Were they truly too busy hating her to pay attention to the small details about her? It hadn't taken Olivia long to pull Caro's lucky number from her memory.

Olivia guessed her luck must have run out.

"Can I get the address of the deceased too? We'd like to search her room and see if there are any indications of something that could have led to her death," McCarty asked. No one responded to the question. Olivia frowned around the room.

"None of you know where she lived?"

"Her driver's license has, well, *this* address, but my understanding is that this was no longer her primary residence," McCarty continued. "If anyone can indicate where she lived..."

"She was staying in a hotel. That's where we picked her up from to come here," Finn finally spoke. "I think she was living there."

McCarty reached in her evidence bag and pulled out a plastic wallet from Caro's purse. She revealed a hotel keycard to the assembled group. "The Sunlight Hotel?"

Caitlin nodded. "That's the one. But... that place was really fancy. She doesn't have a job as far as I know, so how would she afford it? She can't even be bothered to renew her license or get a car. How would she be living out of a hotel?" "Well, looking on her phone... I can see that she has made a number of calls to the hotel over the past few years. Maybe she is a regular there after all."

Olivia shook her head. How had none of her family kept track of Caro's life enough to know where she lived?

"Who was her last call?" Olivia asked. McCarty checked the call log on the phone.

"She made a twenty-minute call to a contact called Anthony Berry. Does the name ring a bell to anyone here?"

Olivia looked around at the blank faces of her family, feeling angrier by the minute. How had they allowed Caro to become so estranged? They'd brushed her under the carpet, just like they had with Veronica when she died. Her uncle at least had the decency to look guilty about it, but Olivia could hardly believe the indifference of them all. Jean caught her eye, gently urging her to stay calm with her gaze, but Olivia looked away. She would keep her anger in check, but that didn't mean she was willing to forgive them. Perhaps if she hadn't felt so unwelcome at the lake house, she would never have gone into the woods.

Perhaps she'd still be alive.

"Would you mind if I accompanied you to the hotel to take a look around?" Olivia suggested to McCarty. "I know we're not officially involved, but I think Brock and I could offer some expertise. I want to find answers as much as you do."

McCarty gave a simple nod. "I don't see any harm in it," McCarty said. "But I want to be clear—this is a murder investigation that my department is handling. You interact with this case at my discretion. Is that understood?"

"Completely," Olivia said firmly. She was more than happy to leave her family behind for a while and clear her head. If she could be of use to the police then she would gladly offer up her time. Someone had to care about what had happened to Caro, even if the rest of her family didn't seem to.

"Keep us updated," Uncle Mark said to Olivia, but she was already turning her back on him and heading for the door. Was he simply trying to keep up appearances? He hadn't cared enough to defend her before, so what had changed?

While the team of deputies took full statements from everyone in the room, Olivia followed McCarty out to her car, Brock following close at her side. He touched her shoulder gently.

"We'll find who did this."

"I hope so," Olivia said, casting a glance back at the lake house. Under that roof, every suspect they had so far was sitting tight, waiting for her return.

Never had she been so anxious to get to the truth.

# CHAPTER ELEVEN

T HE SUNLIGHT HOTEL WAS A HALF-HOUR DRIVE FROM THE lake house, and Olivia was shocked to see how beautiful the place was as they pulled up outside. Marble pillars held up the porch area of the hotel, and golden light came from inside the lobby. The place exuded elegance and money. Olivia tried to pair it with her wild and wonderful cousin, but found that she couldn't. It didn't seem like her kind of place, and yet she was seemingly a regular here. Olivia still couldn't understand how she afforded to stay there, but she was sure she was going to find out soon enough.

Olivia and Brock followed McCarty inside, where the beauty of the place continued on. An elegant chandelier was strung from the high ceiling, casting dazzling patterns of light off the marble floors etched with gold. Expensive red velvet sofas were set in front of a marble fireplace, filling the place with warmth. There were several couples lounging on them, drinking wine in expensive suits and cocktail dresses, though it was still early afternoon. The more Olivia saw of the place, the more she could imagine Caro there, lapping up the luxury and playing the rich socialite. But it still didn't explain how she afforded to join in the lifestyle.

McCarty headed straight for the reception area, armed with the keycard to Caro's room. A handsome young man stood behind the reception area wearing a crisp white shirt and a golden tie that complimented his dark skin, along with a name tag that proclaimed his identity as 'Mikey'. He smiled pleasantly as they approached the desk.

"Good afternoon. How can The Sunlight Hotel help you today?"

"I was hoping to speak to you about one of your guests," McCarty said quietly, showing first her badge and then the keycard to the man. "Caroline Knight."

"I can't give you any information about our guests," Mikey said with a slight frown. Then he clocked the keycard. "How did you come to have Caroline's keycard?"

"I am here investigating her death," McCarty said, keeping her voice low. "She was found dead this morning near her family's lake house. And unfortunately, it wasn't an accident."

The young man's expression turned to horror. His professional smile had slipped and he clapped a hand over his mouth, covering his trembling lip. "Oh my god!"

"I understand she was a long-term guest here," McCarty continued, her eyebrows knitted together. "I'm sorry to bring you bad news, but it's vital we get into that room to see if we can possibly figure out who did this to her."

Mikey's eyes met McCarty's, and then Olivia and Brock's, and after a moment, he nodded in understanding. He wiped a tear from his cheek.

"Please follow me. I'll take you to her room. And I might be able to help you."

70

"Thank you," McCarty said to him. He rounded the desk and ushered them to follow him, wiping at his eyes as he walked them to the elevator. He pushed the button numbly.

"I'm sorry to be unprofessional. It's just that...Caro was a good friend of mine," he said, his voice choked up. "Ever since she moved in here, we've been talking every day. She is...she was a very sweet girl."

"She was," Olivia said with a nod. "She's...my cousin."

Mikey looked up at her thoughtfully. "Olivia?"

Olivia's eyes shot up. "Yes. How...?"

He smiled sadly. "Like I said, we were pretty close. She would talk about you sometimes. Her cool FBI cousin."

A new depth of despair settled into Olivia's stomach. "We had no idea she was living here...we're trying to figure out how she afforded this lifestyle. We only reconnected yesterday...I don't know much about her life, or what she was doing. But her sister said she's unemployed."

"Well. Not exactly," Mikey replied.

The elevator opened up and he led them down the hallway to Caro's room. It was clear that every room on offer was huge, with large gaps between each suite. They approached Room 1313 and Mikey turned..

"I know that in recent years, she has kept her distance from her immediate family," he told Olivia. "She never really said why. But I guess if you're unaware of what she does for money, I can understand..."

McCarty swiped the keycard and opened the door, and the group. She was shocked to find the place bursting with Caro's energy. Her clothes were strewn everywhere, endless amounts of *stuff* filling the room.

Olivia was surprised to see a veritable shrine of wealth and luxury in Caro's suite. Designer handbags were arranged in a row on the dresser behind several bottles of expensive perfume. Dozens of pairs of high heels, boots, and shoes were piled up in a corner, and the closets were practically bursting with clothes that ran the gamut from elegant cocktail dresses to hip streetwear.

"How did she afford all this stuff?" Brock wondered aloud. But Olivia, turning a trained eye to her surroundings, noted that more than anything else, Caro owned quite the collection of lingerie. In fact, it seemed she owned more of it than anything else.

And then she saw the camera tripod set up in the corner, set up to face the king-sized bed, golden sheets neatly made to perfection despite the messiness of the rest of the room. Olivia's breath caught in her throat.

"Is that what I think it is?" she asked.

"Yes, I guess this might be a shock to you," Mikey said, scratching his chin in discomfort. "Caro's work was kept very discreet by the hotel...we don't judge here. In fact, many of the staff have been involved in her...content. She wasn't short of admirers...or clients."

Olivia could barely believe what she was seeing.

"She sold her...content online?"

"Yes," Mikey said. "But she makes a lot of money through it. Some of the guests would be involved in it too, but mostly, it was just of herself, as far as I know. There are people all over the world who would pay a lot of money to see a woman as beautiful as Caro."

"You sound close to her," McCarty said, an edge to her tone. Olivia could tell what she was implying. But the young man seemed unfazed.

"We all loved Caro. And yes, I admired her beyond a friendship. We were intimate, and we made content together sometimes. I'm not ashamed of it, I see no reason not to tell you. But I always understood where we stood. We were never exclusive, not in the slightest. She meant a lot to me, but I would never hold her back. No one could pin Caro down. Only a fool would try."

Olivia stared around the room, allowing Caro's reality to settle in. She had no idea that Caro would lead a lifestyle like this. But she wasn't utterly surprised at the notion. Caro was always a free spirit. She never had boyfriends, at least not ones that she kept, and she had never been able to hold down an ordinary job. It all seemed to make sense now.

But a life like hers could be dangerous. Exposing her life and her body online, making money from men whose lust fueled her career and lifestyle. It invited jealousy and obsession into her life. Was that how she had ended up dead in the forest? Had one of her admirers taken things too far?

"I...I had no idea about all of...this," Olivia said. The young man nodded.

"I'm sorry you had to find out this way. I know she kept her life very private from those who knew her before. I don't think she wanted to be judged. She knew her family wouldn't approve, of course..."

"I don't judge her at all," Olivia said. "I'm just... I wish she would have told me. This could all have put her in danger. And it opens things up a lot. Anyone could have taken their obsession with her too far... it's been known to happen."

The young man nodded. "Yes, I understand. There were risks involved. But I assure you, the hotel made sure that Caro was taken care of. She was safer here than anywhere. She wasn't the only one living in the hotel who dabbled in such a career. Many of the staff also had connections with her. It was well known and accepted around here. That's part of the appeal of this hotel for many. And I assure you, we keep an eye on the regulars here. Any signs of trouble and they are exiled."

"Does the name Anthony Berry mean anything to you?" McCarty asked. "He was the last person she called before her death last night."

The young man winced at the reminder of her death. "Yes, I know Anthony Berry. He comes to visit her here regularly. But he was one of her more discreet visitors...he's a married man. Not that it's uncommon for married men to come to see Caro. Women too. She had a lot of lovers."

"What exactly was the nature of Caroline's work? Was she a prostitute?" McCarty asked bluntly. The young man shook his head.

"No. She made online porn, which was hidden behind a paywall. She worked with clients to create videos online for her subscribers. Some of her admirers would come just to watch her work. Some of her lovers partake too."

"And can you think of any of these... lovers that might have taken things too far? Perhaps they wanted to hurt her because she was seeing other people?"

The young man hung his head. "Not that I can think of. It comes with the territory of this nature of work. There was an understanding, more or less, that being with Caro was a privilege. She had far too much independence to stick to one person. And too much love to give."

"I know she was close with my other co-workers, even... some of the men on the bar staff loved her just as much. And she was very close with her personal security guard. If anyone can help, I think it would be him. His name is Eddie. He's off duty this weekend, given that Caro is away... he'll be devastated to hear what has happened."

Olivia's throat was sore from the effort of holding back tears. She had to admit it was odd to hear the man speaking about his intimate relationship with her cousin, but it was also touching to know she had such an effect on so many people. She was loved here, admired in a way she wasn't in her family circles. It tugged at Olivia's heartstrings, knowing that at least she was appreciated in other areas of her life.

McCarty nodded. "Thank you for your help. We might need to question you further later... but for now, can we take a look around the room? We need to see if there's anything that could indicate what happened to the victim."

"Of course. I want that as well," the man said. He nodded respectfully to them before leaving the room. Olivia could hear his sobs from down the corridor and she pressed a hand to her chest to hold back the pain of it all. She had a task to complete, and she couldn't allow her grief to stand in her way.

McCarty handed Olivia and Brock a set of gloves each.

"I assume you know crime scene procedure," McCarty said. Olivia nodded. She didn't like to relinquish control, especially given that this case was personal, but she also knew she was lucky to be involved at all. This was McCarty's case and she wasn't going to stand in her way. For now, she had more important things to focus on anyway.

It wasn't going to be easy looking through Caro's things, and not just because it was an emotional task. She seemed to own a lot of stuff, likely gifts from her admirers and random things she had bought because she had more money than sense. It made Olivia feel both affectionate toward her and pained, knowing she had had it all ripped away from her. She longed to take a step back, to breathe and feel the agony of it all, but she didn't want to fail Caro. She had no intention of stepping aside when she wanted to see justice for her cousin. So she began to sort meticulously through the room, looking for anything that might be an indicator of why she had been killed.

It was clearly going to be an all-day job. Olivia found herself rooting through endless bags looking for evidence, examining hundreds of papers that Caro had never gotten around to sorting, turning the room upside down in search of anything that could be important. But three hours into the search, it was Brock who nudged her, holding out a crumpled piece of paper to her.

"You might want to read this," he murmured to her. Olivia took the paper from him. It looked like a love note, and it wasn't the first they'd found. It seemed Caro's lovers were traditional, putting their thoughts on pen and paper rather than shooting her an email. Perhaps it had something to do with the fact that the lovers she had seemed to be older men, from what they'd found so far.

"She's got a lot of love notes..."

"This one is different, trust me," Brock said, his expression grave. Swallowing back her nerves, Olivia looked at the paper.

*Dearest Caro,*

*You can't ignore my affections forever. You know you belong to me. You always have. The rest mean nothing to you, but you have always loved me, always trusted me. Don't turn your back on me just because you're confused about what you want.*

ELLE GRAY | K.S. GRAY

*Don't think I'm just going to stand back and let you walk away from me. Don't think I'll stand by and watch those other men try to have you. I need you, and you need me, even if you don't know it yet.*

*I will burn everything to the ground for you. Take this as your last opportunity to make things right. I won't ask again.*

Olivia's blood ran cold. The letter was unsigned, but Olivia was sure that whoever had written the letter could be their killer. How could they not be? It was a threat disguised as a love letter, walking the line between passion and violence. Had Caro been scared when she read the letter? Or had she laughed it off as she so often did with anything serious. Had she told anyone about the note? Probably not. She always felt that she could fend for herself. But now she was dead, and they were too late to do anything about it.

With shaking hands, Olivia handed the letter over to McCarty. She watched the sheriff's face turn from curiosity to fear, glancing back at Olivia in horror.

"Well, this is as solid a lead as any. I'll see if we can pull any prints off it. Whoever wrote that letter had the potential to hurt Caro. It might lead us straight to our killer."

Olivia nodded. She was glad for McCarty's perspective on this case. Because if it was up to her, she would tear down the entire town until she found the monster who wrote that note.

# CHAPTER TWELVE

66 I THINK WE ARE FAR FROM DONE HERE," OLIVIA TOLD McCarty as they headed back through the hotel lobby. "By the sounds of it, there were a lot of people working in this hotel who had a close relationship with Caro. I'm not totally comfortable knowing that most of them had some sort of sexual relationship with her... but I don't think we can leave until we speak to them all. The nature of their relationships invites a crime of passion."

"You're right," McCarty said with a nod. "I'd like to talk to the bar staff in particular. We know for sure that some of them had a relationship with Caroline. If you don't feel comfortable attending the interviews, I can arrange for a deputy to take you back to the lake house..."

Olivia shook her head. "No. I need to be here. I want to help. And I don't think we should stop with the bar staff. We have to consider that her security guard might know something. Sounds like he'd been protecting her for some time, and the moment they were separated, something awful happened to Caro. Maybe he might be able to fill us in on suspicious characters in her life."

McCarty nodded again. She seemed grateful to have Olivia and Brock as backup on this case. But Olivia was more than happy to help her if it got them answers quicker. It had only been a few hours since they found Caro's body, and the weight of her loss was threatening to crush Olivia already.

McCarty led the way to the hotel bar and Olivia fell behind with Brock. He placed a gentle hand on her back.

"Are you alright?"

Olivia nodded, unable to speak for fear of bursting into tears. She had to at least pretend that she was handling this okay, but it was a hard pill to swallow, especially on the back of Jonathan's funeral. She wished she could just curl up in bed and cry until she felt a little better. But she knew the only way she would be able to move on was getting answers. She had to be stronger than she felt. She had done it a million times before. She could do it again.

The hotel bar was just as stunning as the rest of the hotel. The marble theme continued and gold furniture was dotted around the room. It was nearing dinner time and the room was filling up with beautiful people in beautiful clothes. Olivia wondered how many of them were regulars, how many of them drank with Caro each evening, how many of them accompanied her to her bedroom. The shock of her lifestyle was starting to wear off a little, but when she tried to picture Caro among the guests, she was already a fading image in Olivia's mind. She blinked away her thoughts and followed McCarty up to the bar.

The tall, thin man working the bar looked forlorn. His eyes were a little puffy and his skin was pale. There was no professional smile plastered to his face, no cheery greeting as they slid onto bar stools. He sniffed quietly as he acknowledged them.

"Help you?" he asked sullenly. Olivia clocked his name badge on his chest—Christopher. Not a name that Caro had mentioned, but definitely one that had appeared in her contact list. It was clear he was one of the men she had been close with.

"I'm sure you've heard the news? About Caroline Knight?" McCarty asked gently. Christopher swallowed, averting his eyes from them.

"Yes, I heard."

"I'm here investigating what happened to her. I was told that some of the bar staff were close with her, and I'd like to talk to you a little, if that's okay?"

Christopher nodded, looking like he might burst out crying if he said anything aloud. *You and me both,* Olivia thought.

"Can you tell me what your relationship was with the victim?"

Christopher swallowed. "It was complicated."

"Complicated how?"

"We...we cared for each other. But Caro cared for everyone, and everyone cared for her in return," he said. Olivia didn't sense any bitterness in his tone, though she searched for it. "I guess our relationship was casual. No strings attached...unless you count the money."

"Money?" Olivia asked. Christopher blushed.

"Well, I earned some money from any content we created together. Caro was making a lot from her work, and she wanted to make sure that anyone she was involved with was paid too. I made more money from her videos than I do working here some weeks, honestly. But it was never about the money for me."

"Did you love her?" McCarty asked shortly. The bluntness of it was like a gut punch to Olivia. Seeing someone being questioned about someone she knew felt strange, especially when she wasn't the one asking the questions. Christopher sighed.

"I don't know. Maybe? We all loved her a little bit. She had that effect on people. But it's not like I expected anything from our relationship."

Olivia nodded. He was the second person who had drawn that conclusion from their relationship with Caro. Did any of them take it further than she allowed them to? It didn't seem so, thus far. Somehow, it seemed like all of the men Caro had chosen were respectful of her position. Maybe she wasn't as reckless in her choices as Olivia had thought.

But it only took one bad guy to slip through the cracks to end her life.

"You seem very accepting of the way things were with Caro. Was everyone the same?" Brock asked. Christopher wavered.

"I mean, it's a little awkward…a lot of the guys I work with had some form of relationship with her. That kind of stopped me making any friends at this job. We weren't exactly in competition, but I guess we all had to share our time with her. It did complicate things…the arrangements caused drama, for sure. Some of the guys would get jealous. Some of them ended relationships for her…or squashed things before they really got started because they wanted to remain in Caro's life. And look, I don't blame them. She was special. But as you can imagine, her way of living wasn't always easy. And for the guys she favored…like me, and Mikey at reception…it was harder. But I always thought it was worth it."

"Can you picture any of these men wanting to hurt her?" Olivia asked, a tinge of desperation in her tone. "I mean, all these complications you've mentioned…do you think anyone here would act violently because they didn't get what they wanted from Caro?"

Christopher considered the question with a frown.

"The thing is…I can definitely see some of the guys getting into fights over her. It's probably happened before. But they would never take it out on Caro. I'm almost certain of that. She always made her stance clear. She didn't want to be tied down, and she wouldn't entertain anyone who didn't respect that. Her boundaries were very clear. So if anyone got mad about their situation, I imagine they'd take it out on one of her other guys, not on her. Look, I can see from your faces that you think the whole thing is strange, and it is, believe me. But this is the kind of hotel where it's considered normal. Everyone here lives their lives a little on the edge, but it's a part of the status quo. And for the most part, things run smoothly. Nothing like this has ever happened before. Caro was safe here…whatever happened to her, it happened away from this place. I think either someone was biding their time, waiting to draw her out…or this is a random act. Women like Caro drive people crazy in all sorts of ways. She should have stayed here, where she was safe."

Olivia rubbed her temple, fending off a headache. This conversation was only making Olivia realize how expansive Caro's network was. Anyone could have a reason to want to hurt her, despite what Christopher was implying. He wasn't the one who searched for criminals as a career. He had no idea the lengths people would go to when driven by the desire to control someone. And by the sounds of it, hundreds of men were lining up for a moment in the sun with Caro. Had she rejected someone and made him angry? Had she let a romance go a little too far and hurt someone's feelings? Anything was possible, but it was going to be like searching for a needle in a haystack looking for someone to blame this time.

"You said that Caro had favorites…" Brock said. "Yourself included?"

"I guess so, yeah."

"Can you tell us the others who were top of her list? Does Anthony Berry ring a bell?"

Christopher sighed. "I don't like the idea of discussing her private life…"

"Nothing is private in Caro's life anymore," McCarty said bluntly. "We have to dig up all of her dirty laundry if we're going to figure out who would want to hurt her. Staying quiet isn't doing her the favor you think it is."

"I'm Caro's cousin. Believe me, I know she'd be more interested in justice than keeping her reputation under wraps," Olivia said gently. "We need to know everything."

Christopher took a deep breath. "Can't argue with that… yeah, I know who Anthony Berry is. He visited her once a week, sometimes twice. On rare occasions he'd spend a week, and Caro was always in a good mood when he did. I think if there was anyone that Caro was likely to fall for, it was him. He's an older guy, in his late fifties…but it was complicated between them. It was strictly personal with him, he didn't like her choice of career.

But he was married, so he lacked the grip on Caro that he wanted. She kept him at arm's length, knowing she couldn't truly have him for as long as he had someone else on the side."

"You're saying that most of the men involved with Caro didn't maintain any other kind of relationships?"

"Pretty much. I think the problem was that Caro kept everyone on their toes…she was so charming and charismatic that it was like…no one else compared."

Olivia still found the whole arrangement odd, but to hear people talking so lovingly about Caro was a breath of fresh air. Did she have any clue about the effect she had on these men? She must have known. Is that why she separated herself from her family as much as she could, knowing she could find love elsewhere that would be reciprocated? Deep down, was Caro just looking for the kind of love that came without conditions, knowing she wouldn't get it from her family? The thought was bittersweet and a little lonely. It made Olivia's throat tighten a little.

"Do you think Anthony felt the same way about Caro?" Olivia asked.

"Oh, definitely. He was obsessed with her. I think of all the guys she was involved with, he worried me the most. Because he didn't respect her the same way everyone else did. He wanted to lock her down, even though he wasn't willing to leave his relationship to be with her. He's that type, you know? The kind that needs control. But she wasn't about to give it to him. She wouldn't give that up for anyone, not even him. But yes, he clearly cared deeply for her."

"Did they ever fight, that you know of?"

Christopher bit his lip. "I don't know. Caro wouldn't really disclose much about him to anyone. She was kind of protective over what they had together. But from what I could tell from the outside, things seemed pretty smooth sailing between them. Like I said, if they weren't both so stubborn, I think they would have been together for real. He was in a different league from the rest of us, even some of her other favorites. But I've got to admit, I haven't seen him around lately. Maybe something happened, I can't be sure."

"Would anyone be likely to be able to tell us more?"

"I think if anyone would know about them having a fight, it would be Eddie. He knew her best, given that she hired him to take care of her. He's off duty this weekend, given that she was going away... I don't know if he's even heard the news yet."

"We're going to need to speak to him," McCarty said. "Can you give us an address where we can find him?"

"You'd be better off asking Mikey. He'll be able to give you details."

"You don't think Eddie would be involved in something like this, do you?" Olivia asked. She didn't want to leave any avenue unexplored. But Christopher shook his head fervently.

"Absolutely not. Eddie's a good guy. And he's one of the few who didn't have a relationship beyond friendship with her. He's always stayed faithful to his wife. He cared for Caro like a daughter... and he kept her safe. He's going to be devastated. I think we all are."

"Thank you for your help," Olivia said earnestly, her voice cracking a little. "To hear someone speaking so kindly about her... it's nice."

Christopher's eyes swam with tears. "Above all, she was a good friend of mine. If I set everything else aside, that's what I'll remember most about her. She was kind and loving and the funniest person I'll ever meet. I don't think I'll ever stop missing her. I'm finding it hard to believe she's gone. I don't think it's set in yet."

"I know," Olivia said. "I guess that's the problem with meeting someone like Caro... it hurts so much more when they're gone."

# CHAPTER THIRTEEN

OLIVIA WAS QUIET ON THE DRIVE TO GO AND MEET EDDIE Burns, Caro's security guard. She was still finding it hard to picture that her cousin had a life where having a security guard was necessary, but it wasn't the thing that was bothering her most.

She couldn't stop thinking about the difference between her family's attitude toward Caro and the men she had been seeing. She had never noticed before just how indifferent her uncle and sister were to her, treating her as more of an annoyance than anything else. Olivia understood that they knew Caro a lot better than she did, and that she did have the kind of personality that could rub people up the wrong way.

But it was just so sad to Olivia that Caro had to seek out love elsewhere, knowing she wouldn't get it at home. Olivia knew all too well that families had cracks within them, but even Caitlin's reaction to Caro's death was cold. Stephanie's too. Her uncle had seemed upset, but even he seemed more interested in keeping the peace with his wife and his other daughter. How had they got into such a situation? How had Caro been left out on the outside for so long that she had to turn to other means for affection?

Olivia had no doubt that Caro had loved her life. It was clear from the way those men spoke about her that she was well loved and that she had the time of her life, indulging in a raunchy and luxury lifestyle. She didn't have to worry about money and she had very little responsibility—wasn't that a life that everyone craved?

But she was also living a completely unusual life, and it was possibly the reason she had ended up dead. Olivia had been quick to lay blame at her family's feet, knowing the tensions that were present there, but now she wasn't so sure. She couldn't rule it out, but she could also read between the lines. A violent death like Caro's wasn't likely to be performed by a woman—Olivia wasn't sure that Caitlin or Stephanie even had the strength to hit Caro hard enough to kill her, even if Caitlin was outside when the crime took place. And while neither of them liked Caro much, was it enough to make them kill her? Sisterly rivalry and a stepmother's distaste wasn't as strong a motive as love or passion.

But then the men Caro took to bed weren't the only ones obsessed with her. Olivia thought back to Finn's wandering eyes, his intense stare, Caro's insistence that he was always that way. But what she failed to see was that he wasn't that way with everyone—not even his girlfriend. It was him that scared Olivia the most, and he absolutely had the means to attack Caro in the forest. Maybe Caitlin had even seen it happen. After all, they were out there around the time Caro likely died. Was it possible they lied? That they saw or heard something, or that they were involved themselves?

Olivia didn't want to dismiss any of it, but she was interested in speaking with Eddie first. As they began to put together the bigger picture of Caro's life, it was becoming clearer that her life had been chaotic. But if there was anything out of the ordinary, Eddie was likely to know about it.

So long as he had no reason to want her dead himself.

The thought made Olivia nervous. He was the one who knew where she was going and when. He had been hired to protect her, but what if obsession had gotten the better of him, the way it had with so many other men in Caro's life?

Olivia gasped as she felt a hand touch hers across the backseat of the car. She looked up and saw Brock giving her a knowing look. The kind of look that told her not to spiral again. Olivia swallowed and squeezed his hand back. Once again, he knew exactly how to keep her feet on the ground.

"We're here," McCarty said, pulling up outside a modest house on a quiet street. The sky was beginning to darken now, and there was a light on inside the house. "I'll take the lead, but if you have any questions, please feel free to make your input. You've been a great help so far. I hope for your family's sake that Eddie will have some answers for us."

"Me too," Olivia said as she clambered out of the car. She followed McCarty up the driveway and they all waited after McCarty rang the bell. A minute passed before Eddie showed at the door. Urgency clearly wasn't on his mind, which meant he didn't yet know what had happened.

He opened the door with a smile. Eddie was a big man with long hair tied back into a ponytail and a protruding gut, with faded tattoos rippling up and down his arms. He looked like he'd once been quite the athlete, but age and beer had softened his physique, and smile lines squinted his eyes. Despite the man's hulking size, he looked like he couldn't hurt a fly. Olivia pictured him as one of those bikers who rides for charity or a backstage technician for a rock band. But his kind smile quickly turned into a frown when he noted McCarty's uniform.

"What's this about, officer?" he asked in a deep, gruff voice. McCarty interlocked her fingers behind her back, clearing her throat.

"I'm sorry to interrupt your evening... but I need to speak with you. Eddie Burns, isn't it?"

"The one and only."

"I've been at the Sunlight Hotel today investigating a case. I'm sorry to inform you that Caroline Knight was found dead earlier today near her family lake house."

Eddie's face crumpled in horror. He clapped his hand over his mouth, making a muffled sound that sounded like he was in pain.

"My Caroline? Oh God ..."

"I'm so sorry," McCarty said, but Eddie was already retreating into his home, away from them. A woman with a full figure and gray hair appeared in the hallway, scowling at the guests.

"What have you said to upset my husband?" she demanded to know. McCarty scratched her head in discomfort.

"I'm sorry to be the bearer of bad news... his client was found dead this morning."

"Lord above," the woman said, shaking her head. "That poor girl. You're talking about Caroline?"

"I'm afraid so."

She looked crestfallen. "Sweet thing. I knew her pretty face would get her in trouble some day. I guess you'd better come inside."

Olivia uncomfortably stepped inside, following the woman into the living room with McCarty and Brock. Eddie was on the sofa, his head in his hands as he sobbed. His wife put her arm around him, soothing him gently though her own eyes held tears. She turned to look at McCarty.

"You'll have to excuse my husband. He was very fond of young Caroline. As was I. A troubled young thing in some ways, but she had a heart of gold." The woman glanced at Olivia and narrowed her eyes. "I know you. You're her cousin, right? She talked about you sometimes. Said you were in the FBI. She showed me pictures of you in the papers. She was so proud of you."

Olivia swallowed back the lump in her throat. It was enough to almost set her off crying too.

"That's so sweet. Caro meant a lot to me. I just wish I had spent more time with her."

"You never know how much time you have," the woman said, rubbing Eddie's trembling shoulders. "She was here for dinner just last week. She told Eddie to take this weekend off, that he wouldn't be needed while she was at the lake house…"

"I knew I should have gone with her," Eddie moaned. "I knew she needed me."

"You couldn't have known," his wife said, kissing the top of his head. "And you know what she was like… once she had made up her mind, she wouldn't change it. She would never have let you go with her."

"Why were you so insistent on going with her? Were you concerned about her safety?" McCarty asked. Eddie struggled for breath, wiping his eyes. He took a shuddering breath and looked up at her.

"I don't think Caro was ever truly safe outside of the hotel. Her online following was becoming too much… men recognized her in the streets sometimes, or would try to follow her home. And the men she chooses… far as I'm concerned, not all of 'em can be trusted. She wouldn't listen to reason, though. I know trouble when I see it, and trouble was always on her horizons."

"We were told that you would be the person to talk to about Caro and her relationships," Olivia said softly. "Christopher at the bar said you were very fond of her."

Eddie sniffed. "I never got to have a daughter of my own… Molly and I took her under our wing. We knew her relationship with her family was… difficult. And we just wanted someone to give our love to. She was like family to us. Yes, she paid me for my work, more than she should, but I know it's because she trusted me to take care of her. I don't think she was used to feeling that way in life. And given the things she got up to, she put herself in some vulnerable positions, for sure. I know everything about what went on in her life."

"And do you think you could tell us where the trouble lies?"

Eddie's face hardened a little. "There were a few guys I had to chase off from time to time… but one of the worst stuck like glue to Caro. She never saw the harm in him."

"Let me guess. Anthony Berry," Brock said. Eddie nodded with an affirming grunt.

"Knew him way back in high school. He was a couple of years behind me, but he stood out to me even then. He broke a few hearts back in the day, but it's different now. He doesn't have any respect, not even for Caroline. He liked her because she kept him on his toes…he wanted certain things from her that she would never give. I just *know* that drove him crazy. It made her want to pursue him more. I told her not to trust him…"

"It sounds like you weren't the only one," Brock reassured Eddie. "We believe you. Do you think…do you think he was capable of killing her?"

Eddie closed his eyes and shook in anger. "I honestly don't know. But I certainly don't trust that man. To cheat on your partner speaks volumes about your character…and he was more committed to Caro than he was to his wife. Tells you a lot, don't it?"

"Did Caroline ever seem afraid to you?" McCarty asked. "Did she express that someone was scaring her? She did receive some strange letters…"

Eddie bit at the skin around his thumb. "She never said she was scared. I know about the letter in question. One of the things she asks me to do is to sort through her mail…she never wanted to read the crudest ones, and she got a lot of inappropriate letters. But I handed her one in particular because I was worried about it…the person who wrote it seemed to be obsessed with her, and acted like they knew each other personally. I worried it might be Anthony. But when I told her to take the letter to the cops, she laughed it off. She said if anything, it was passionate. I think she liked the attention."

"That sounds like Caro," Olivia said, her throat sore and cracked. Eddie shook his head, sad and affectionate in his action.

"She told me to toss it in the trash, but I put it with the others. I felt it would be important someday. I did think about taking it to the cops myself…but I knew she would see that as a betrayal of her trust. And I figured it wouldn't matter…anyone who wanted to get to her would have to get through me first, and that was never going to happen. I should have been there at the lake house with her…"

"You couldn't protect her forever," Molly said, rubbing Eddie's back. "She was a free spirit. She told you she needed time away from it all. We could never have expected this…"

"I'll never forgive myself," Eddie said solemnly, his face crumpling. "I was supposed to take care of her…"

"Please don't blame yourself," Olivia said softly. "You looked out for Caro when no one else did. I know that would have meant so much to her. And the only person at fault is the sick person who decided to hurt her. You can't take responsibility for that."

"Whatever I can do to help…please, let me help," Eddie sobbed. "I'd do anything to get answers for her."

"Me too," Olivia whispered. "Me too."

# CHAPTER FOURTEEN

Anthony Berry lived in a mansion fit for a king. It was all white stone and big columns holding up the porch, with a driveway that could fit at least five cars. The problem was that the house was behind a giant set of metal gates. Olivia sighed. Why did her work always seem to land her on the doorsteps of people with more money than sense?

"I bet he's not going to feel like coming out to talk to us," Brock said, voicing Olivia's thoughts. She shrugged.

"Either he complies now or we come back with a warrant. But I'm not in the mood to wait around for him. If anyone knows something, it's him. His name keeps cropping up, it can't be a coincidence."

"I know you want answers, but we've got to be careful. We can't afford to let emotions stand in the way."

"I'm not," Olivia snapped. Then she paused and hung her head. "Sorry. I guess I am, a bit."

"It's okay. I get it. This isn't easy. But if we blow this, we won't be allowed to stay on the case."

"I know," Olivia said. She took a deep breath. "Okay. McCarty can lead the way. I'll stay back and try to make some judgments about Anthony."

Stepping out of the car, Olivia and Brock met McCarty by the gate. She seemed to be attempting to navigate a complex intercom system. She grumbled, jabbing a few of the buttons impatiently.

"Damned rich folk," she muttered under her breath. "Nothing's ever simple with them."

The intercom suddenly crackled to life, making McCarty jump a little. A dramatic sigh came from the other end of the call.

"Would the three people standing at my gate care to explain what the hell you're doing here?" a male voice drawled. Olivia glanced at Brock, raising an eyebrow. It seemed this cocky man was either unbothered by Caro's death, or he might not be aware.

"We would be more than happy to explain if you open the gate," McCarty said. A snort came from the man.

"Nice try. I don't just let strangers into my house, do you?"

McCarty pulled her badge and presented it to the camera. "I know you can see this, wherever you are. I'm investigating a murder, and let's just say that I've heard the name Anthony Berry cropping up a fair few times today. Can you think why that might be?" McCarty asked coldly.

There was a long silence on the other end of the line. "A murder? Who died?"

"Someone you were very close with, according to multiple sources. We can discuss this further inside."

Anthony fell silent. But after a few moments, the gate began to open before them. McCarty sighed, ushering Olivia and Brock to follow her.

"Let's leave the car outside. I want to get in there before he changes his mind. Any initial thoughts?"

"He seemed cocky when he first picked up the call... but his mood definitely shifted when you mentioned murder. Maybe he feels cornered... or maybe he had no idea someone was dead. It's hard to tell which is more likely before we've even seen him. But he's going to be a tough nut to crack," Olivia said. Ahead of them, the door to the house opened and a man stood before them. He was dressed in a blazer and a crisp white shirt, an odd choice for inside his home, Olivia felt.

But Anthony Berry had clearly made a reputation for himself. And showmen always came prepared.

Anthony glared at the three of them as they approached. He stood tall, his chin jutted.

"You better have something good to disturb me like this," he said. Olivia looked him up and down, wondering what on earth Caro saw in him. He was tall and slim, his hair graying a little, and he had the type of mustache that Olivia had to assume was meant to be a joke. But Anthony himself seemed very serious, and she wouldn't be surprised if his facial hair was treated with as much seriousness. Olivia wondered why Caro would choose someone like him to fixate on when she could clearly have anyone she wanted. Was it the money? Was it the thrill of knowing he was married? She would never find out now.

"I think we do," McCarty said. "We're here to investigate the death of Caro—"

"Don't even *think* about finishing that sentence," Anthony hissed. "Her name is forbidden in this house."

Anger swelled inside Olivia. "She's *dead*. And you're worried about speaking her name? Why? Worried that your wife will overhear and get mad about your affair again?"

Anthony's nostrils flared. "Who the hell are you to speak to me that way?"

"I'm an agent in the FBI. And I also happen to be Caroline's cousin. So you should be very, *very* careful about how you speak to *me* moving forward, Mr. Berry."

Anthony's mouth fell open, but he composed himself quickly. Olivia could see Brock smirking in the corner of her eye. He might have told her to behave, but if Anthony didn't plan to, then neither did she.

"I suggest you get your priorities straight and give us the answers we're looking for," Olivia said, pushing past him into the house. "This doesn't need to be difficult."

Olivia felt satisfied by Anthony's obedient silence, but she also felt anger burning in the pit of her belly. How did this heinous man dare to care more about keeping the peace than the death of his lover? It had been his choice to sleep with Caro, to carry on whatever relationship they had. Now he was trying to sweep her under the rug, hardly even caring that she was gone forever, only trying to save his skin. Olivia had been suspicious of him before, but now she was just blinded by hatred. She promised herself that she would keep to the sidelines for the rest of their time in Anthony Berry's home, but her anger remained. She knew it would take a long time to go away.

She tried to hold herself together as they followed Anthony through his house. Looking around her, Olivia could see the appeal for Caro—the lavish lifestyle was something she clearly never shied away from. But did she ever step foot in this place, or did Anthony just always seek her out? How could they be in a real relationship when she'd never even been allowed to set foot in his home? When she was kept a dirty little secret from the world? It made Olivia feel ill. Didn't Caro understand that she was worth more than that?

Now she'd never know.

The thought only stoked her fire. As they entered what Olivia was sure was one of many living rooms, Anthony wordlessly invited her to sit down and she did, wanting to curl up into herself to stop her fury from bursting out. Brock sat down beside her and placed a gentle hand briefly on her knee. It was a comfort, but also a warning. He knew she was close to flying off the handle, and she'd promised him she'd keep her cool. She breathed in deeply and avoided looking at Anthony. It was easier that way.

He too sat down, though McCarty stood by the ornate fireplace, clearly too riled up to sit and talk to a potential murderer. McCarty's face was hard as she looked at Anthony.

"Nothing to say about the news you've just received? Any words about the woman you've been seeing for... two years, now?"

Anthony sniffed, his face blank. "It was purely sexual. We weren't in a relationship. And I don't want to see you looking at me like that, Agent. We had an arrangement and she knew what it was. I don't need your judgment."

"And you're telling me that you have no emotional response to a person you've known... very intimately being found dead? She was murdered," McCarty said bluntly. "Perhaps you know something about it? You didn't seem surprised."

Anthony leaned back in his chair, his fingers threaded together. "What do you want from me? It seems to me like you're gunning for a confession. I haven't left the house all week. My wife and I have been spending some time together. I haven't seen that girl in some time."

"How long, exactly?"

"Some time," he repeated vaguely. "When my wife found out about her, it was game over. I saw her once more and not again since."

*Game over.* Olivia tossed that phrase around in her mind, feeling more and more irritable. Caro was just a conquest to him, one he surely thought he had won. Did it please him, knowing that he was the one Caro had wanted the most, but he never felt the same?

"So this was the first you were hearing of Ms. Knight's death?"

"I found out earlier. Local news. I guess I was prepared for a visit from the police," Anthony said solemnly. "All roads lead me back to her. She became the bane of my life, a complication that I had little control over."

"I doubt that very much, Mr. Berry. I suspect it's you that has little control, considering you were the one having an affair, not Caroline. That sounds like a choice to me," McCarty said. Olivia felt a rush of warmth for her new acquaintance. She was glad someone had spoken up against Anthony while she had to remain silent. At least she knew someone was defending Caroline.

Anthony pursed his lips. "She had an effect on me, I'll admit. It's been a rough few years in my marriage. We've been together so long. Things can get stale. And Caroline was… enigmatic. But as I said, she became troublesome. Clingy."

"I can't imagine why. Perhaps it was the game of cat and mouse you were playing with her," McCarty sniped. "Or the letters you wrote to her?"

Anthony frowned. "Letters? What letters?"

"No recollection of the love notes you sent her? The passionate, intense words that told her she belonged to you and no one else?"

"I've never written Caroline a letter in my life. I was having an affair. Do you really think I would leave a paper trail?" Anthony snapped. Olivia curled her lip in disgust. He really was vile. But he did seem genuinely surprised at the notion of a letter. Perhaps he wasn't the writer after all.

"So you never tried to take any ownership over her?"

"Absolutely not. Not in any real sense," Anthony said. "Sure, there's things that we said to one another in the bedroom… but let's be real, the closer we got, the more trouble I was going to be in. I was toeing the line already and I had no intention of making things harder on myself. Caroline had trouble written all over her."

"Will you stop talking about her like that?" Olivia snapped. "As though she alone was the cause of your problems? *You did this.* Take some ownership over the mess you made, for crying out loud."

Anthony smirked at her. "You wouldn't understand. You're too young. One day when you're not young and gorgeous you'll look back and kick yourself for giving me a hard time. When you've been married for thirty years maybe you'll rethink your stance."

"When I've been married for thirty years I'll be thanking the stars that I had someone to commit to for so long," Olivia said. Brock gripped her leg again and she swallowed back her next angry retort. Maybe it had been a mistake to come to Anthony's house. But as she sized him up, she didn't want to keep her mouth shut. How was it that everyone around her got hurt? That everyone she knew suffered in some way they didn't deserve? It was like everything she touched turned to ashes on her fingers.

"Here's the thing, Mr. Berry," McCarty said, pulling the focus back in her direction. "We already know you're a liar. You've lied to your wife, the one person you're supposed to always be honest with. What's to say you won't lie to us about what you know?"

"Because I'm not stupid enough to draw attention to myself this way," Anthony countered, rolling his eyes. "I've already got an angry wife to deal with twenty-four seven. You really think she's going to let me out of her sight right now? I'm practically under lock and key. You think I can possibly sneak out to see my younger lover and then *kill* her? Is that what you're implying? You realize how stupid you sound, right?"

"And yet yours is the name on everyone's lips," McCarty fired back. "So don't try to gaslight us. That might work on your wife and on Caroline, but it won't work on us. If you're so innocent then explain to us why three separate people suggested we speak to you about Caroline's death?"

Anthony fell silent. McCarty raised her eyebrow.

"Well? No answer for that one?"

"I have the right to a lawyer," Anthony said coldly. "And I won't say anything again until I have one at the ready."

"You do realize how suspicious that makes you look?" Brock said. "Innocent people aren't clamoring for a lawyer the second they're under the spotlight."

"You're just trying to rattle me now, but I won't allow it."

"We can apply for a warrant and search your house. Is that what you want?" McCarty pressed. "I'm sure your wife will love that… watching us turn your house upside down in the name of the woman who destroyed your marriage."

"Do it, then. Get a warrant. Search the place top to bottom. Just get out of my house until you have a real reason to be here. And see how much you find," Anthony snarled, his words a challenge. Olivia stood up, her hands curling into fists.

"We'll be back," she said. "I hope for your sake you have nothing to hide."

# CHAPTER FIFTEEN

"**D**O YOU WANT TO TALK ABOUT WHAT HAPPENED BACK there?"

Olivia was sitting in the passenger's side of McCarty's car as she drove them back to the cabin by the lake. The last thing Olivia really wanted to do was return to the scene of the crime, the place where everything went wrong, but she knew she would have to face up to her family at some point. They'd have questions and she wouldn't be able to give them answers. She closed her eyes, pressing her forehead against the cold window.

"I know I was unprofessional. I let my feelings get the better of me. But he's a piece of work. I couldn't help it."

Brock nodded. "Don't get me wrong, Olivia, I always love seeing you put an idiot in his place... but that could have really compromised our case."

Olivia groaned. "I know."

Brock hedged for a minute. "Now, I'm not... I'm not saying that you can't handle this. But is it possible that you might need a step back?"

Olivia opened her eyes again. She could tell that McCarty was listening to their conversation, though she kept her eyes on the road and her posture stiff. Olivia didn't feel like admitting her shortcomings in front of this woman she'd just met, but Brock had put her on the spot a little. She sighed.

"Maybe this whole thing is not the best idea. I can admit that. But I'll go crazy if I don't try to help. I feel so... guilty."

"What have you got to feel guilty about, Olivia?"

"About a million things. How about the fact that I just watched her walk away into the forest alone? We've been in this job long enough to know that's almost always a recipe for disaster in the middle of the night. And then there's the fact that I didn't keep in touch the way I should have. I've learned so much about Caro today... stuff I never expected. She had this whole other life that she never shared with her family... and I feel awful about that. She didn't have anyone she could turn to. No one to rely on..."

"Olivia, you're her cousin, not her mother. You're not responsible for her, or what happened..."

"I know. I know that deep down. But I just wish... I just..."

"I get it," Brock said, placing his hand over hers on the backseat. "But you can't live like this. You take too much on. You know better than this. Whoever wanted to hurt Caro was just waiting for their perfect opportunity. They planned ahead for this. There's nothing you could have done."

Olivia's throat felt tight. She knew that Brock was right. She couldn't see the future. She could never have known that Caroline's lifestyle would have her on a risky path. She'd never been given the full picture, and she was still far from piecing it all together. And yet, a knife still twisted in her stomach. A chill still rested on her spine. How could she shift that feeling when someone she'd cared for was dead?

Olivia thought of her sister at that moment. Her death had gone unsolved for so long. It had been a sour taste in Olivia's mouth and a dark shadow over her days. It had taken her so long to claw back out of that dark place, and now she could feel a force trying to drag her back into the abyss. Jonathan's death was heavier than it had been hours earlier too. Olivia understood all too well that life was full of loss—you could never hold on to something forever. But lately, she felt that everything was slipping through her fingers, the sands of time speeding up beyond her control. And without control, what did she really have?

"Why don't you sleep on it?" McCarty suggested after a long silence. "You can spend the night with your family, allow yourself some time to grieve … and then maybe you might feel more ready to be involved. Your insight will certainly be helpful to the case, so I would hate to lose you. I need all the help I can get."

"You seem very capable to me, Sheriff," Olivia said honestly. It was McCarty who had kept their interview with Anthony Berry on the right track when Olivia was struggling to stay afloat and keep her cool.

"That's kind of you to say. But everyone can use a little help every now and then. I don't want any slip-ups. I want justice for your cousin too," McCarty said gently. "And please don't worry about how you conducted yourself earlier. I also liked seeing you give that smarmy hole a piece of your mind. No one needs to know."

Olivia sighed. "We didn't get much out of him …"

"On the contrary … you made him put his guard up, wouldn't you agree? He went on the defensive, and that's usually the sign of a guilty man. Perhaps he needed to be prodded a little to give away his true colors. And once we get a warrant, I can get my team searching that place head to toe. Don't beat yourself up. You're human. You're allowed to feel your pain."

Olivia nodded, unable to speak, but she felt grateful for the sheriff's kindness and grace. It wasn't often she was told that it was okay for her to be emotional. Her line of work demanded the kind of hardness of a person that was almost impossible to achieve. She knew that Brock felt the strain of the pressure too, sometimes. When their cases entwined with their emotions, it made it ten times harder.

But Olivia had to remind herself that when times get hard, she also gets stronger. There was no denying that she'd walked through fire many times before, but she wasn't afraid to get burned anymore. Her pain would carry her through every single time.

And that's how she would get justice for Caro.

It wasn't long before they arrived back at the lake house. McCarty caught Olivia's eye in the rearview mirror.

"Take it easy tonight. Call me in the morning and we can rendezvous. But if you need some time, feel free to take it."

"Thank you," Olivia said, sliding out of the car. As soon as she shut the door, she could hear raised voices from across the yard. She glanced at Brock, who raised an eyebrow.

"I bet we can guess who that is."

Olivia gave a curt nod. She had no doubt that they were hearing an argument between Caitlin and Finn. Given that they'd been out in the middle of the night, Olivia still felt suspicious of them both. Neither of them had a steady relationship with Caro—Caitlin's jealousy and Finn's wandering eyes made for the perfect breeding ground for trouble. As McCarty's car backed quietly out of the driveway, Olivia was grateful that their arrival was incognito. She ushered Brock to follow her to the edge of the house.

Inside, Olivia spied her uncle and mother sitting in the kitchen, talking with their heads bowed. They were clearly otherwise occupied. Caitlin's voice was carrying on the wind, a harsh, raspy whisper from the other side of the building.

"What the hell am I supposed to do, Finn? If you hadn't been so…so…*obsessed* with her then no one would be looking our way."

"Me? Take a look at yourself, Caitlin. You're the one blinded by obsession. You're too wound up in your hate that you can't even consider the fact that you're the obvious suspect. You'd do anything to get rid of her."

"She ruined my life. Just by existing. She took everything I ever had or wanted. And you added fuel to the fire. You *promised* that you didn't want her, but I could *see it*. You think I'm stupid, Finn? Because I promise you I'm not. You should have left me a long time ago."

"I'm beginning to think the same. You're insane. You're shifting blame to me, but how am I supposed to trust you? If someone asked me who did it, I know for sure who I would think of first."

Olivia's heart skipped a beat. Were they really standing there blaming one another for Caro's death? And if so, did that mean that they didn't work together?

Whatever the conversation was about, it was clear that their relationship was just as rocky as Caro had implied. And Olivia had to admit that Finn's words rang true. His obsession with Caro was full of lust, but Caitlin's was born of hate, and it had been growing since they were children. Who had more reason to want her dead?

"You've crossed one too many lines," Caitlin said, low and threatening. "You'd better make a decision fast. Are you on my side or not?"

A chill ran down Olivia's spine. She had heard malice in her cousin's voice plenty of times. She always knew how to play the villain throughout their lives—always the one desperate to spoil the fun, the one ready to put someone down and stomp on their happiness. But this was different. This was something darker and more personal. A threat of a different magnitude.

And Finn's silence spoke louder than any words could.

"Fine. I see how it is," Caitlin hissed. "I'll get through this alone. Like I always do."

Olivia heard her retreat inside the house. She looked at Brock with fear in her eyes. She didn't want to believe that Caitlin could do something as cruel as killing her own sister. And yet it didn't look good for her. She was out in the forest when Caro died. She had a motive and she had the means.

All she would need was the perfect opportunity.

Olivia and Brock waited silently in the dark until they heard Finn follow Caitlin inside. Only then did Olivia allow herself to breathe.

"What do we do?" she whispered to Brock. "That sounded... well, it sounded bad."

"It's not enough to go on. We need more context. But you're right. I don't think we can trust either of them right now," Brock agreed quietly. "In fact... I'm not sure who we can trust, realistically."

"My parents, of course," Olivia said. "But no one else. What do we tell them when they ask?"

"Omit the details, but tell the truth. That we don't know anything yet. That we'll keep looking."

Olivia nodded firmly. They couldn't afford to give away what they'd heard. If they did, they might even be in danger. For now, they had to live under the same roof as her untrustworthy family members. She would need to play her cards right if she didn't want to throw herself into danger too.

She headed to the front of the house a few minutes later, leaving enough of a gap in time that her cousin wouldn't grow suspicious of her overhearing them. Brock followed behind.

Inside, everyone's heads turned to them in anticipation. Stephanie clutched her husband's arm, her eyes shining.

"Oh, Olivia. Any news? What did you find?" she asked. Olivia was surprised to see that she looked sincere in her concern. Olivia swallowed.

"Nothing yet," she said, trying not to give anything away. The last thing they needed was a cross-examination. She glanced at Jean across the room, and her mom nodded subtly. She understood not to push the line of questioning. Did she have suspicions too about the intentions of the people in the room? Not one of them knew Caro through and through. Not one of them had been close to her. They'd all failed her in their own ways.

But one of them might have gone the extra mile. One of them might be the reason she was dead. It didn't bear thinking about, but it was too terrifying to ignore. Who wasn't in their bed when they should be? Who snuck out in the middle of the night with the intent of hurting someone who shared their same blood?

Could it be Stephanie, the unloving stepmother?

Could it be Uncle Mark, the indifferent father?

Could it be Finn, the lustful brother-in-law?

Or would Caroline's own sister kill her in cold blood?

It was at that moment that Olivia knew she would return to the case the following day. She had to. She had insight to the family dynamics that no one else did. She could investigate from the inside. She hoped that none of them would be found guilty. But if they were, then at least she would be able to figure it out. She didn't want to make eye contact with any of them as she headed up to her bedroom to rest.

She couldn't look at the people she once trusted the same anymore.

# CHAPTER SIXTEEN

O LIVIA BARELY SLEPT THAT NIGHT. IT WAS IMPOSSIBLE to rest knowing that the last time she'd closed her eyes, her cousin had been brutally murdered not far from where she rested. Guilt twisted in her stomach, making her feel nauseous. Eventually, at four-thirty in the morning, she rose, leaving Brock sleeping. Coffee would have to substitute for a good night's sleep.

The cabin was quiet as the rest of the family slept. Olivia tried not to be too noisy, though the old coffee machine rumbled as it prepared her beverage. Half asleep, Olivia put two slices of bread in the toaster, feeling as though she was on autopilot.

She knew the day ahead was going to be tough. Maybe even tougher than the day before. Reality was starting to sink in and

Olivia knew that nothing was likely to be the same in her family again. She thought of Caitlin's words the night before. *You'd better make a decision fast. Are you on my side or not?*

Those words seemed to hold so much weight, to the point where it scared Olivia. Why did she need Finn on her side? What had she done that was so bad that she needed to request his unshaking trust? Why was she so insistent to have him on her side when he had clearly let her down so many times in the past?

She didn't want to believe that Caitlin was capable of killing Caroline. For all of their sisterly bickering, surely she loved her deep down? Surely she wasn't *glad* she was dead? Surely she wasn't the one who'd done something so horrific?

And yet she had always been the jealous type. She had always hated Caroline's ability to sweep so easily through life, to always have the sun shining on her while Caitlin stayed in her shadow. Even Olivia could see that growing up. Not many people got to stand in the sun with Caroline, but she had never minded so much. Caitlin, on the other hand, had no way to escape it. Caroline was too deeply entwined in her life, and always would be.

Until now, of course.

But then there was one other thing that stuck out to her from the conversation she had overheard between Caitlin and Finn. Something Caitlin had said that Olivia had been turning over in her mind over and over again. *I'll get through this alone. Like I always do.*

That comment wrenched something deep inside Olivia. There was so much pain loaded into those words. Did Caitlin really believe she had always been alone? Could she not see that her family supported her more than they ever supported Caro?

But maybe that was the problem. Caro was the troublemaker—always in the spotlight for all the wrong reasons. And that still kept anyone from looking in Caitlin's way. Olivia couldn't imagine how it must feel to be in her shoes, knowing that her boyfriend only really stuck around to ogle her sister, knowing that Caro was always the topic of conversation even if she was never being praised. Olivia knew she would be distraught if Brock had taken an interest in Veronica over her. She'd spend the rest of her life wondering why she wasn't enough. Why was she deemed the second option?

And now she understood Caitlin a little better. But she knew one thing for certain—no matter how she and Veronica battled in their lives, there was never hate present between them. Veronica could light a fury inside Olivia like no one could, but she saw that as sisterly love. What could sisterly hate do to a person?

What had it done to Caitlin?

The coffee machine finished rattling, leaving Olivia with a mug half filled with coffee. She took it eagerly. Some coffee was better than none. She turned to walk to the living room, but a small yelp left her body when she turned and saw Finn standing in the doorway to the kitchen. He smirked, leaning against the doorframe like a heartthrob in a teen movie, but Olivia simply felt uncomfortable by his sudden appearance.

"Don't spill your coffee," he said. His eyes scanned Olivia up and down and she found herself taking a step back, revulsed by the attention. Caro had been right about him—he was a creep. What Caitlin ever saw in him, she had no idea.

"You startled me," Olivia said bluntly. "You shouldn't be sneaking around like that. Not after everything..."

"You should have heard me coming. Isn't your job not to be snuck up on?"

"My job is to catch creeps red-handed," Olivia said bluntly. Finn seemed unfazed by the dig, or perhaps too stupid to pick up on her disgust with him. He offered her a lazy smile.

"I'm sorry. I didn't mean to startle you."

"That's fine," Olivia said, her guard very much still up. She didn't trust the guy, and she had no intention of giving him any impression that she did. "You're up early."

"I'm a night owl. I don't like to waste the best parts of the day. It's nice and peaceful, I'm usually on my own. I guess I wouldn't mind a little company every now and then, though."

"I was just going to head back up to bed..."

"Stay a while. We're practically family, aren't we? We should get to know one another a little. Especially since everything has gone so horribly wrong..."

"I don't imagine you'll stick around much longer, will you?" Olivia said, cocking her head to the side. "I don't see what you've got to gain from this family any longer."

Finn raised a challenging eyebrow. "Why are you so cynical of me, Olivia? Have I done something to upset you?"

"It's my job to be cynical, as you so kindly pointed out. And no, you've not done anything to me. Not personally, at least. But I think anyone who looks for long enough can see the damage you've done in this family."

"I have no idea what you're talking about."

"I'm sure you don't. That would be convenient."

"Say it with your chest, Olivia. Say what you think of me. I must be so awful for you to have such a negative opinion of me. So why don't you spit it out?"

Olivia met his eyes as a challenge. She was certain she could hold out longer than he could. Did he really think he could walk into their family and ruin it without facing any consequences? Gone was the flirtatious look in Finn's eyes, replaced by something defensive and angry. Olivia held her breath, wondering what he was capable of. If he tried anything, she would be ready for him.

The toaster popped in the background, but Olivia didn't flinch. She didn't want to give him even a second to get the jump on her. She didn't trust him, but she refused to fear him too.

"What's going on here?"

Olivia's eyes snapped behind Finn's looming figure to see her mom appearing from upstairs. She didn't look concerned just from her expression, but Olivia knew her mother better. There was a look in her eyes that told Olivia that she could sense the tension Finn had brought to the room.

"Nothing at all. Just catching up," Finn said with an unconvincing smile. Olivia kept her face level and stony. She had nothing to say on the matter. Not in front of him, at least. Jean pushed past him into the room, her presence unassuming, and yet bold all at once. She tended to have that effect on people. She offered Finn a surface-level smile before turning her back on him to move to the coffee machine.

"Well, I suppose there's plenty to talk about. Strange that you were out there at the time Caroline was killed and you didn't hear anything, Finn."

Finn narrowed his eyes at her. "Like I said. Caitlin and I went on a walk."

"Perfect time for it… two o'clock in the morning. Perfectly ordinary time to head out, isn't it?"

"You sound like you're accusing me of something."

Jean smiled again. "Oh no, not at all. Just commenting. It's my job to be curious too, Finn. I think if anything is amiss, Olivia and I will spot it eventually. Brock too. So there's no need for accusations. Just thinking aloud."

Finn's eyes darkened. "I guess I'll leave you to it."

Jean didn't even flinch. "I think that's best."

Finn glared one last time in Olivia's direction before he skulked out of the room. Jean, unbothered by the interaction, continued to prepare herself a coffee.

"Good thing I'm an early riser," she said. Olivia leaned against the kitchen counter.

"I would've been fine on my own."

"Oh, I know. But I suspect if he tried to wind you up any further, he might end up with a bloody nose. Not what we need right now."

Olivia managed a small smile, though she had to admit the interaction had left her feeling more anxious than ever. She hung her head.

"Nothing feels right."

"I know."

"I can't… I can't believe any of it. And I can't believe I have to question who I can trust."

Jean reached out and rubbed Olivia's arm. "You know better than most that trust is earned. You don't have to give it to anyone you don't want to. Not even family. Though I hope those rules don't apply to me."

"You know they don't."

Jean squeezed her arm again. "Good. And just so you know… I don't trust him either."

"And Caitlin?"

Jean wavered. "I don't know."

"I heard her talking to Finn last night. They said things that made me nervous. But we had a lot of leads yesterday. I can picture a lot of people wanting Caro dead... it's just that Caitlin seems to have a better motive than most."

"You'll figure it out, one way or another," Jean told her. "We just have to hope that the obvious suspect isn't the real one."

# CHAPTER
# SEVENTEEN

A FTER HER ENCOUNTER WITH FINN BEFORE THE SUN HAD even risen in the sky, Olivia felt that it was best to steer clear of her family for the day. She texted McCarty and said that she wanted to return to the woods to do a little investigating. So after a quick, silent breakfast, Olivia and Brock slipped out of the cabin and headed into the trees in silence. Olivia knew it would be difficult returning to the spot where it happened. They walked the path she had walked so many times as a younger woman. A path that had once been full of happy childhood memories was now stained with blood and misery.

She held her breath as she approached the yellow tape surrounding the area where the body had been found. Olivia didn't want to picture Caro lying there, her head bloody, her eyes vacant. But there was no real way to escape that. That image wasn't going to be scrubbed from her mind any time soon.

"You alright?" Brock asked as Olivia bent down to examine the ground. She shrugged her shoulders.

"No. Not really. But I'm ready for the day, if that's what you mean."

"Funnily enough, no, that's not what I meant, Olivia. I'm trying to check in on you."

Olivia rubbed at her tired eyes. "Sorry. Of course you are."

"You've got a lot going on. I'm worried about you."

Olivia sighed. "Between losing Jonathan and losing Caro… I have to admit I'm on the edge. I haven't felt this awful in a long time."

"I know. It must feel… familiar."

Olivia nodded, a lump in her throat. It was nostalgic in the worst possible way—reminiscent of the days after Veronica was brutally killed. It was easy to imagine that their family was cursed, that they had no control over their own destinies.

"You look tired," Brock said softly. Olivia let out a small chuckle.

"Gee, thanks."

"Are you sure you shouldn't be at home getting some rest?"

"I appreciate you trying to help… and I love you for it. But there's nothing you can do for me now. Other than helping me to solve this problem. Then maybe I can rest easy."

"Noted. I won't push you," Brock said. Olivia felt a rush of warmth for him. She appreciated that he didn't push the matter further. He respected her enough to know the time and place for that. "Where's McCarty today?"

"She and her team are doing a deep dive at the hotel. But I said we'd start out here. Since we're not technically on the case, I thought I would give her some space to do her work. And I figured I might have some insight she doesn't have out here… something that could prove useful." Olivia straightened up, looking around her. The copse of trees was dense and repetitive, but as Olivia looked up at the tree before her, familiarity swept over her. It was a large oak with a wide base, roots weaving in and out of the ground like thread through fabric. It stood out from the other trees, and Olivia couldn't believe that her grief had blinded her to where Caro had been found the day before.

"It didn't occur to me yesterday... but this place in particular was a big part of our childhood. Right here by this tree."

"Oh really? I bet you got into trouble out here, didn't you?"

Olivia smiled. "Not me so much. Definitely not Caitlin either. But this tree right here... it was Caro's favorite. She used to bring us here for 'secret meetings' away from the adults. I'm sure they knew where we were, but it was like being in an exclusive club. It made us feel special whenever we came out here. But Caro loved it the most. She always insisted on us coming out here just so we could hang out at the tree. She broke her wrist climbing it too. Fell right from the top. But she still kept coming back here. She loved it."

"So you think it's significant that she died here?"

Olivia chewed her lip. "Possibly. It can't be a coincidence, right? She came here because it meant something to her... but someone also knew how to find her here."

"You're saying that it could be Caitlin."

"I'm saying it's possible. She was out here at the time, in the middle of the night. She saw Caro walking away into the woods, the same as the rest of us. We know how much she hated having Caro around... and that conversation she had with Finn is something I just can't shake off. She didn't exactly paint herself in an innocent light, did she? And then there's something else that's occurred to me. Aside from the two of us, would anyone else really know the significance of this place? I don't imagine she brought anyone else here. Which means it would have to be someone who knew about this place."

Brock's expression turned anxious. "You could well be right. But it's still too loose of a connection for us to really get anything from it."

"Maybe... but maybe not."

Olivia ducked underneath the yellow tape and lay on her stomach on the ground.

"What on earth are you doing, Olivia?"

"Looking for something that the police might've missed," Olivia said. She edged forward a little in an army crawl, diving her hand deep into the roots of the tree. She knew there was something down there, buried low under the tree. Olivia couldn't quite remember where Caro had buried her treasure trove, but she had a hunch that if it was still there, it would give Olivia exactly what she was looking for.

Her hands grappled blindly, soil gathering underneath her nails and cold, wet mud piling up in her way, but she kept searching. She hated not knowing what her hands were touching. She had had enough nasty surprises in her life to feel cautious. But she had to do it for Caro. She had to follow her hunch all the way if she wanted answers.

Her fingers brushed something cold. She grabbed on to it, awkwardly bending her arm to shuffle the item out of hiding. When she triumphantly freed it from the tree roots, she laid eyes on something she hadn't seen in a long time.

"What is that?" Brock asked. Olivia smiled.

"A time capsule. Caro's," she said. She turned the tin box over in her hands. On the base, engraved in pristine handwriting, were the words *Caroline Knight*. Olivia took a deep breath. "I have this feeling that there's something inside."

"But why?"

"Because anyone who knew Caro well would know about the time capsule. And someone that knew Caro *and* wanted her dead ... might consider this a good place to hide a murder weapon."

Brock's mouth fell open, staring at the box. Olivia almost didn't want to open it up. She knew what was in the box— photographs from their childhood, Caroline's first lipstick, an empty bottle of vodka that Caro had stolen when they were teenagers, a love note that she'd never sent to a boy in her class. Olivia had been there when she packed all those memories away and stuffed them under the roots of the tree.

But the box had a weight to it that Olivia was sure it shouldn't have. There was something in there that shouldn't be, tainting those memories. Olivia swallowed. Anxiety twisted her stomach.

"I have to take a look," she said aloud, more to herself than to Brock. With slightly trembling fingers, she undid the clasp holding the time capsule together. When it popped open, she lifted the lid to reveal the contents.

Sitting atop Caro's memories was a rusty hammer.

Nausea squeezed at Olivia's stomach. The hammer looked like it had been well used, but not for DIY projects. Blood the color of rust was evident on the handle and the metal of the apparatus. Olivia didn't touch it, knowing that it was going to be needed as evidence. She swallowed down her emotion and snapped several pictures of the box before investigating further. But even as she did, a dark truth settled into her stomach.

Someone had known where to find the time capsule and hid the weapon that killed Caro there.

"Olivia?"

Olivia took a shaky breath. "I... I think Caitlin could have done this. She was there the day Caro hid the time capsule. It was just me, her, Caro... and Veronica. I don't know who else would be aware of where to find this."

"But would Caitlin be stupid enough to hide the weapon somewhere that meant something to you all? Surely she would guess that you'd look here?"

Olivia's throat was tight and she shook her head in disbelief. "I don't know... I really don't know right now. If this was a crime of passion, a spur of the moment thing... then perhaps she panicked and hid it there. It meant something to her too... killers often hide things in places of importance to them. But why would she have a hammer with her unless it was planned? She's not exactly the kind of woman who carries tools around with her. I don't think she's ever used a hammer in her life."

"But someone she knows uses one every single day," Brock pointed out. Realization dawned on Olivia. A hazy conversation came back to her, one where Caitlin's boyfriend told her that he was a contractor...

"Finn," Olivia whispered. Brock nodded solemnly. Breathless, Olivia closed the lid of the time capsule. She couldn't bear to look

ELLE GRAY | K.S. GRAY

at the weapon any longer. She met Brock's gaze and saw her own fears reflected in his eyes.

"So if they were both out here at the time of Caro's death ... and they both had a reason to want her dead ... was this premeditated? Did Finn leave the cabin with the intention of wanting Caro dead and gone?"

"It's entirely possible. So far, both of them have some pretty convincing reasons to want her out of the way. And after the conversation we overheard..."

"It feels possible," Olivia breathed. The more she thought about it, the more convinced she felt. But she knew that it wasn't enough for them to have some pieces of their puzzle fitting together. To get the whole picture, they'd need to send the hammer off as evidence and dust it for fingerprints. Finn and Caitlin weren't exactly trained killers—if they'd done this, it was amateur hour. They might have made mistakes, left their mark on the murder weapon...

They'd have answers in no time.

But this was personal. Olivia's anger wasn't something she could contain for that long. She had to talk to them both. She had to dig them out for answers. If they were innocent, then they'd have nothing to hide. But if they were guilty?

She would get them to confess.

# CHAPTER EIGHTEEN

THE WALK FROM THE FOREST BACK TO THE CABIN FELT longer than it should have. Olivia was driven by her new-found anger, a hateful feeling burning hot in every fiber of her being. She prayed that she would be wrong, that the hammer wouldn't belong to Finn, that Caitlin didn't have so much hate inside her that she'd be willing to let someone kill her sister. But out of all their leads that they'd found, this one felt the closest to answers. And every clue, every piece of evidence, seemed to point in the direction of Finn and Caitlin.

They were sitting on opposite sides of the living room when Olivia returned. Olivia's uncles Mark and Jared were sitting with them, and a few others had filtered into the living room, but none of them appeared to be talking to one another. They jumped a little as Olivia slammed into the house.

"What's with you?" Finn scoffed. Olivia's heated gaze turned on him.

"Maybe I should be asking you that question."

"What's going on?" Mark asked, confused by Olivia's sudden angry appearance. She held up the time capsule box pointedly.

"Recognize this, Cait?" Olivia asked. Caitlin got to her feet, looking unsettled at the sight of their childhood memory box. She backed off a little, like she knew what it might hold and what it might mean for them. For *her.*

"What are you doing with that old thing?" she asked. "I thought Caro buried that under the tree years ago?"

"She did. And you were there when she did. It was just you, me, Caro and Veronica. I doubt anyone has seen it since," Olivia said. "So maybe you can explain to me why this is inside it."

She opened the box with a flourish, revealing the bloodied hammer. Caitlin stepped forward to peer inside the box, then recoiled with her hand covering her mouth.

"Is that…"

"The weapon used to kill Caro? It seems that way. And what I want to know is how the hell it got there. This box was buried beneath Caro's favorite tree, right where she died. Only we knew about it, Caitlin. So did you put it there? Or did you tell your boyfriend where to stash it?"

"Olivia!" Uncle Mark snapped. "I don't know what you think you're implying, but that's quite enough."

"I'm not finished," Olivia said darkly. "I have to ask these questions. It's my job. You know that this looks bad. Why was it that Caitlin and Finn were out in the middle of the night and they claim not to know anything about this? There's only two people alive who knew where that box would be—me and Caitlin. And you, Finn? You're the one with an extensive toolkit for work. Did you keep this hammer to one side to do your dirty work? Were you so desperate to have Caro that you made sure no one else ever would again?"

"You're messed up in the head!" Finn cried at her. "You're supposed to be some kind of hotshot detective and you're blaming me for this? You've lost your damn mind. If you don't back the hell off, I swear to God..."

"What? You'll kill me too?" Olivia asked coolly.

"Enough!" Caitlin cried. "This is ridiculous. I won't hear any more of it, not in front of my family. Olivia, outside, *now.*"

Olivia's cheeks were hot as she paused her tirade. Caitlin strode toward her, grabbing her arm hard and pulling her back into the yard. Olivia tried to pull from her grip, but Caitlin's fingers dug deeper into her skin, hard enough to bruise. For a moment, Olivia felt a flicker of terror. She knew Caitlin was hot-headed. If she was a killer too, what was she capable of doing to her? Had she made a mistake with her approach?

Caitlin pulled them to the edge of the water before she whirled around to face Olivia. She was breathing hard, but there was no anger in her eyes. In fact, there wasn't much of anything at all in her gaze. She took a deep breath and then exhaled slowly.

"I'm going to need you to take a breath," she said to Olivia. "And tell me what the hell just happened back there. This isn't like you, Olivia. Surely you don't actually believe any of what you're saying?"

Olivia took a step back from her cousin, her hands gripping the box tight. Holding the box almost felt like protecting Caro, even though she wasn't around to protect any longer.

"Don't gaslight me right now. I'm not sure what I believe fully yet, but I had to follow my instincts. All the signs are pointing at you and Finn, Caitlin."

"What *signs?* I don't know what you're talking about!"

"Don't play dumb. You were sneaking around in the middle of the night when Caro was killed. And it's no secret that you hated her. You've never had a good thing to say about her. You've been actively trying to get her out of your way for your entire life."

Caitlin bristled. "So you think I killed my own sister just because she and I didn't get along? I'm pretty sure you need more than that, Olivia. Though you should know that. You're the FBI agent, not me."

"I know more than you think. I heard you arguing with Finn too. The context might not have been fully there, but even Caro had her suspicions about Finn. She told me as much. You knew he was being inappropriate with your sister, wanting something he couldn't have from her. I can see how that could drive a person to madness. So did it, Caitlin? You have the motive and the means, and between you? It seems even more likely. You were the only other person who would know where to find this box, and the pair of you—"

"*Enough,*" Caitlin snapped a second time. "I've heard enough from you, Olivia. I'm going to put this outburst down to an emotional break because believe me, we're all feeling the strain. I might not be crying and raging, but I'm not finding this easy either. I'm just trying to keep my cool. But if you keep coming for me I'm really going to get mad."

"You know I have to play this out, Caitlin. You look guilty as hell right now, do you understand? I'm doing my job. I'm trying to get justice for your sister."

"I'm *sick to death* of people going on about her!" Caitlin screeched. Olivia blinked at the outburst, taking a step back. Caitlin's fingers pressed against her temple and she let out a stressed sigh, shaking her head to herself.

"Sorry. I'm not coping well with all of this. Better than you, maybe, but not well," Caitlin said. She swallowed, tears appearing in her eyes. That was enough to shock Olivia back into reality. She wasn't sure she had ever seen Caitlin cry. She'd always appeared to be less emotional than most, preferring to give way to crueler emotions like anger and jealousy than sadness. It was odd to see her crying. Caitlin dabbed at her eyes with her sleeve.

"Look...I get it. I know you must think I'm this horrible, evil cow. I haven't shed a tear for Caro since I found out the news. I must look like I've never once cared about her. But you've got to understand something...the girl was the bane of my life. She treated me like a second-class citizen ever since we were kids. And everyone outside our family unit worshiped the ground she walked on. You did too. But I'm here to tell you now that she wasn't who you thought she was. At least, not the version of her I knew."

Caitlin shook her head. "She was so selfish and self-centered and cruel. She knew that the way she acted always shunted me to the side, and she did it anyway. I was never allowed to have anything. Not just when we were kids, but when we grew up too. I got so tired of it, tired of *her,* tired of no one being able to see her the way I did, the way Dad did too. She was spoiled rotten and I just couldn't ever forgive her for the person she chose to be. And now she's gone… and it's still all about *her.*"

Olivia's forehead furrowed in anger and confusion. "She's *dead,* Caitlin. Someone killed her. Of course it's about her. What the hell do you want us to say? You want us to forget her when she's not even in the ground yet? You don't want us to try and find out who killed her? What's wrong with you?"

Caitlin put her head in her hands and shook it. "I don't know," she moaned. "I just don't know…"

Olivia forced herself to take a few steadying breaths. They wouldn't get anywhere by shouting at one another, that much she knew. And now that Caitlin was trying to give her defense, she owed it to her to listen. Caitlin's lip trembled as she lifted her head back up.

"I am sad she's gone. I swear I am. But in the most selfish way it's also a relief. I wouldn't expect you to ever understand. You and your sister had your moments, I'm sure, but I know you loved Veronica. And not just because you were told to. Your love was unconditional. Mine came with a list of rules and regulations that Caro seemed insistent on breaking. She trampled over everything I did, every effort I made. She stole anything that I tried to make for myself…"

"Are you talking about Finn?"

"And every other boyfriend I've ever had. Do you know how hard it is knowing that every boy I've ever given my heart to only wanted me so they could ogle her? I was a gateway to something they could never truly have, but at least they felt one step closer to heaven when they had a reason to be around her. They never really loved me for me. Finn included. And I learned to live with it ... but it's like living with a knife in your back, constantly twisting itself inside you. It hurts so bad. And the worst thing is ... it wasn't always her fault. She was never actively going after my partners ... she wasn't that evil. She just had a way of making people love her without any effort. I couldn't bear always being the second or third or fourth choice. I just, for once, wanted to be the one someone chose. And I never got to that point."

"And you think she stole Finn."

She shook her head. "No. I saw for myself that she rejected him. I caught him a year or so ago trying it on. She said no. But that's the problem. She didn't need to do anything to make that happen. It just did. I've spent years hating her for being the beautiful one, the confident one, the passionate one. And in return, she defended herself against my anger, as she had the right to. And in the process, she humiliated me even further. She reminded me that I'm the inferior one, the cruel, boring, ugly, undesirable version of her that no one wanted. She had no idea how deeply it hurt me. It made me despise her and everything she ever did. Every time I saw her, I burned myself to the ground again and hoped that someday, I'd drag her down with me."

She turned away and took a deep breath before continuing in a low voice. "That kind of hate is impossible to live with, Olivia. It made me hate myself even more than I hated her. And I don't want to feel this way, but I do. I can't escape it, even now. But even after all that, even with everything she ever did to ruin my existence, I *still didn't kill her.* And I'll tell you why you can trust my word. Because if I had the guts, I might have done it. I could have strangled her some days. I could have really really gone in on her, because she brought out a rage in me that only she knew I possessed. I would never want to kill her, but I think if she'd pushed me much further, I could maybe have done it. Except I knew how it would end up. She's got even more power now than she did when she was alive. She's some kind of martyr. Everyone brushes the things she was under the carpet and remembers her bright presence, her unrelenting talent, her beauty that's just going to be immortalized for the rest of eternity. She'll never grow old and ugly." Caitlin scoffed, almost choking on it. "She'd love that. She'd be so pleased to know that she'll forever be young and beautiful. Desirable and unattainable as always. What a joke."

Olivia felt cold to the core at Caitlin's speech. She had never realized just how deep Caitlin's hatred for her sister ran. It had carved her out into the most hateful creature. She was everything Olivia had thought she was when she walked inside and accused her of murdering Caro.

And yet she still insisted that she didn't kill her sister. The person with the most reason in the world to want her gone was still trying to claim her innocence. Was Caitlin simply wearing her heart on her sleeve for once, or was she lying to get out of everything she'd done? Olivia had no idea if she could trust her cousin's words. Her honesty was chilling and hurtful and dark. But if it was all true, if she was willing to admit her darkest desires, did that make her trustworthy? She'd laid herself out so fully that it almost seemed impossible to believe.

Caitlin's eyes bore into Olivia's. "You think I'm crazy. I can see it in the way you look at me. Don't worry, I'm used to it by now. And I get exactly where you're coming from. I'm the ideal candidate for the killer. I hated her more than anyone on this earth, and I had more right to than anyone. But I didn't do it. I would never. And even my hate couldn't make me believe she deserved this. To die like that, alone and afraid... I wouldn't wish that on my worst enemy. And I know that because she's dead now, and despite it all, I wish she wasn't."

Olivia hung her head. She had no idea if she could trust Caitlin's words, but she didn't have anything solid to pin her yet. And now, she understood Caitlin in a way she hadn't before. In a way that terrified her. Olivia raised her head to meet Caitlin's hard gaze.

"She felt alone too, you know."

Caitlin scoffed. "Sure."

"She might have been loved by everyone else, but she was never given a place in this family. Your dad didn't give her any love. You said it yourself, he saw her the same way that you did. I don't know why, but not being cared for by your own father? Don't you think that was hard for her? Stephanie rejected her too. You hated her guts. She had to go looking for love elsewhere and I don't think she ever truly found it. Everyone saw her on the surface and never wanted to look any deeper. And I get why she inspired so much hate, especially in you. She had everything you wanted, and she even took things from you that you thought you already had. But did you ever consider that you were both fighting for the same things? The things the other had that you never did? Don't you think you both deserved to be happy?"

Caitlin's eyes softened ever so slightly. Olivia watched her throat bob as she fought back tears. She glanced away from Olivia, trying to keep her expression neutral even as it wobbled.

"Then why did she never say anything?"

Olivia looked at Caitlin with sadness in her eyes. "Why didn't you?"

The comment seemed to choke Caitlin. Her hand moved to her throat and she turned toward the water. She stood there for a long time and Olivia felt frozen in time with her, the pair of them coming through their anger slowly, then all at once. Caitlin's shoulders heaved as she steadied her breath.

"I'm only going to say this once more," she said, her voice hoarse now. "I didn't kill her. I don't think Finn did either. I'm not saying that because I trust him. He cared too much for her to ever do it… and it's like you said, we were together at the time." She went quiet for a moment and then she scoffed, shaking her head to herself. "I can't believe you humiliated me in front of our family like that… but I guess I shouldn't be surprised. You always did dote on her."

"Don't try and guilt me for trying to solve a murder, Caitlin. Even if I'm inclined to believe everything you just told me, I don't trust you. You've just proved to me exactly why I shouldn't."

"Maybe you're right. Not many people tend to trust me. Everything I do is tainted by my jealousy, clearly. That's how the world sees me. I know that now," Caitlin said coldly. "But you can take that hammer away and do your thing. You won't find any evidence against me because I didn't harm a hair on that girl's head. But I'm not surprised that someone did in the end. Karma comes for us all."

Olivia clutched the box in her hand a little harder. She didn't have much left to say to Caitlin. She supposed she would have to speak to her eventually, but she had to prove her guilt if she wanted to take this any further. She turned on her heel, considering going back to the house to deal with the fallout of her outburst. She had no idea what she might say, but at least perhaps she could smooth things over.

"Wait."

Olivia turned around to see Caitlin looking at her. Her eyes were red and raw, like she'd finally managed to shed some tears. But her voice was steady when she spoke.

"I think I might know something useful," Caitlin said. "A few weeks ago, I got a call in the middle of the night. It was Caro. She left a voicemail that I ended up deleting. I thought it was just a drunk rambling…"

"What did she say?" Olivia asked, her heart pounding. Finally, something that could be of use to her. Caitlin swallowed.

"She said she thought she was being followed. That she was scared. I tried to call her back the next day when I heard the message, but the number was dead. She must have gotten a new phone. She was always getting new phones. I tried to bring it up on the drive over, but she laughed it off. She clearly didn't want to confide in me a second time."

"Did she say who she suspected was following her?"

"Not exactly… She said she felt like it could be someone she knew. Someone who was obsessive over her. But like I said, she brushed me off after that. She wouldn't talk to me. And I didn't want to mention it in case I got in trouble. But it seems I never stood a chance. The fingers were always going to be pointed at me."

"Then you'd better hope that you're innocent," Olivia said coldly. "Because if you did it, I will arrest you myself."

# CHAPTER
# NINETEEN

T HERE WAS A FROSTY ATMOSPHERE AT THE CABIN. THAT
was to be expected, given that Olivia had all but accused
Caitlin and Finn of murder. But the family had split itself
down the middle. While Jean, Roger, Brock, and Olivia kept
close to one another, Caitlin stuck with Finn and her father,
her stepmother clinging to him too. Much of the rest of the
family seemed unsure what to do or who to side with, so they
kept their distance. But as far as Olivia was concerned, she
had every right to be suspicious of Finn and Caitlin. Despite
Caitlin's insistence that they had nothing to do with Caroline's
death, Olivia had decided to think of her as guilty until she
was proven otherwise. Caitlin had said it herself—she was the

one with the best motive to want Caro dead. Everyone else seemed to adore her. Why would they want her dead?

But Olivia knew they had to explore every avenue. Until she could hand the weapon over to the police and find solid proof, Caitlin and Finn were free to do as they pleased. That's why when Olivia received a call from McCarty asking if she'd like to assist with searching Caroline's messages, she agreed right away. She needed something to keep her occupied, and out of Caitlin's way. The family were still due to remain at the cabin until the end of the day, but Olivia had a feeling that none of them would be leaving until more information was found. At least, Olivia hoped not. She couldn't afford to let Caitlin and Finn slip away. If they were guilty and had any sense, they'd use it as an excuse to run.

"Will you keep an eye on things here today?" Olivia asked her mom as she headed out to Brock's car. Jean put a gentle hand on Olivia's shoulder.

"I will, don't worry. No one will be going anywhere."

"Good. We can't afford to let anyone leave yet. Not until we know more."

"Do you believe that Caitlin might have done this?" Jean asked her. Olivia sighed.

"I don't know. She hated her so passionately that I can picture her doing it. An awful thought to have. But Caitlin has never been a violent person. Not the Caitlin I know. Yes, she had a temper, but in a mild kind of way. It doesn't seem in her nature."

"I agree," Jean said softly. "Which means that it's best to keep a lid on things for now, don't you think?"

Olivia sighed. She knew Jean was referring to her outburst earlier in the day. She hung her head.

"I know. I'm not feeling myself at the moment. I'm just so... *angry.*"

"I know."

"It feels like the whole world is against me sometimes," Olivia said, her words catching in her throat. Jean pulled her close to her chest.

"Olivia... you're always on the path to self-destruction. You know that you do that to yourself, right?"

Olivia chuckled quietly. "Yeah, I can see that."

"I'm saying this to you as your mother, as someone who cares about you deeply. Give yourself a break. Not everything is your fault. Not everything in the world weighs on your shoulders. And whatever has happened here… it's not on you to make it right. I know how anger can cloud your judgment. And I get it. I don't feel proud to be a part of this family right now either. But work with the facts. Get the right answers. Everything else is irrelevant. You're a great agent. You've never let anyone down yet. I trust you'll make it work."

Olivia nodded solemnly as her mother kissed her on the cheek.

"Put your anger aside, if you can. Then your instincts will serve you well."

"And I have you to guide me too," Olivia said softly. Jean cupped her daughter's cheek with a gentle smile.

"That you do. Always."

Jean headed back inside and Olivia got into the car feeling right on the edge of tears. Brock put a hand on her knee.

"She really gets you, doesn't she?" Brock said. Olivia sniffed.

"Sometimes. Not always."

"More often than you realize, I think. You're both very alike. I bet she understands the way you feel right now. She went through it with Veronica too."

"I hadn't thought of that," Olivia said. Whenever her judgment was clouded, she felt like Brock helped clear the skies for her. He started up the car, backing out of the driveway.

"She's looking out for you. I hope you know I am too."

"Of course."

"Good. Now, let's get on with some detective work. Forget this morning. We can hand the time capsule over to the police and get cracking with Caro's phone. Something tells me it'll be a goldmine. All those people she knew, all those people who were obsessed with her… if there's something to find, it'll be on that phone."

"Maybe. Caitlin told me that she disconnected her phone a few weeks ago, though. The phone found on her body can't be very old. We might be missing some vital information."

"It's possible. And we'll never get back the voicemail Caro left for Caitlin… but if she had other worries, maybe she reached out to another friend… or a lover."

"It's strange. Eddie didn't mention that she was being stalked, did he? So if she didn't mention it to him, who else would she tell? He was one of her most trusted friends from what we've gathered so far."

"Maybe she didn't want him to worry. He seemed protective… maybe a little suffocating for a free spirit like Caro. Her phone will be the key, I'm sure of it. It's the place where she'll get honest with people and allow herself to be vulnerable. She likely found it easier to hide behind a phone and to release her anxieties there. Maybe it made it feel less real to her."

Olivia closed her eyes and tried to think of the brief time she'd spent with Caro on the night she died. She hadn't seemed like a woman on edge, someone scared of being stalked or hunted down. She seemed carefree. But then again, that was Caro. Could any of them really, truly read her?

"I think it's more likely that she brushed the whole thing off. That she decided not to worry about something she couldn't control," Olivia said. "She was tough. She wasn't about to let a few creepy messages slow her down. It's like Eddie said about that creepy letter she received… she just told herself that it didn't matter."

"But it likely did," Brock said. "The letter was possessive of her… that might work if we can connect it to Finn, but not Caitlin. She wanted little to do with her sister, I doubt she would send her a letter like that. So if the killer and the writer of that letter are the same person… then I would rule Caitlin out."

Olivia nodded, but said nothing else. She couldn't trust Caitlin for even a second, but even she had to admit to herself that it was Finn who worried her more, despite his affection for Caro. Lustful obsession could be a dangerous thing. But in terms of their suspects, there could be hundreds of men willing to take

129

their obsessions to a new level. And for now, Caitlin was offering Finn an alibi. It was possible that they'd have to look elsewhere. She hadn't forgotten about Anthony Berry either. It seemed that everyone in Caro's life had trouble written all over them. But one of them had killed her, and they'd have to be sure before they could point fingers properly. Olivia hoped that McCarty would have something of use for them so that they could wrap the miserable case up and try to return to normalcy.

They met McCarty at the hotel again, but the place seemed very different than it had the last time Olivia visited. The place had been cleared of guests and staff, replaced by police cars in the parking lot and officers milling around the lobby. Olivia found McCarty upstairs in Caro's room. This too had been cleared, with many of her items taken in for evidence. There was barely a trace of her left behind, and it made Olivia's chest hurt. But she pushed those feelings aside and greeted McCarty with a firm handshake.

"Thank you for inviting us to join you again," Olivia said politely. McCarty gave her a curt nod.

"I'm glad you're here. You said you had something for us?"

Olivia handed her the box she had found in the roots of the tree. She kept her face stoic as McCarty carefully opened the box.

"We found the murder weapon, we assume. The box was Caro's time capsule from years ago. Only a handful of people would have known where to find it… it was buried in the roots of the tree where she died. It only occurred to me when I started thinking straight that we played there as kids."

"So the place meant something to her?"

"And to Caitlin. She was there when Caro buried the time capsule. Only me and my sister knew about that… but my sister is dead now."

McCarty frowned. "I'm sorry to hear that." "Seems our family is a little cursed," Olivia said dryly. "But anyway… Caro must have gone back there because it was familiar to her. And whoever killed her knew she would be there, and where to find the time capsule. Unless she told someone about it, it looks like Caitlin is carrying guilt."

"Looks that way. But we'll need to take the hammer in as evidence and see what we come up with. And in the meantime…"

"The phone."

"Yes, the phone. Think you could take a look at the messages this afternoon?"

"Sure. Anything to help."

"I'll process the evidence. Good find with the time capsule. Hopefully it'll give us the answers we're looking for."

McCarty left Olivia and Brock behind in Caro's room, slipping the phone into Olivia's hand as she left. Olivia stared down at the screen for a few moments, feeling the weight of everything the device could contain. It could give them the answers they needed to solve Caro's death, but Olivia was sure that each message would weigh heavy on her heart. Her conversation with Caitlin earlier that day had made her feel odd about her love for her cousin. Was she really as terrible as Caitlin had insinuated? Yes she was wild, yes she was known for taking center stage and never sharing it, yes she was sometimes oblivious to real life unfolding around her.

But she wasn't uncaring. She had a lot of love to give—anyone who truly got to know her could see that. Did it matter if she was always the star of the show? Not to her.

But she felt a pang of guilt for Caitlin. She'd been so passionate in her hatred for Caro and it had changed her to the point of no return. Her life had been so overshadowed by her sister that a life without her was preferable to her. Olivia had never once wished Veronica dead. She'd do anything to have her back. How could anyone see death as anything other than a loss?

"Do you want me to take a look?" Brock asked Olivia. She blinked, realizing that she had been staring at the phone for some time. She shook her head.

"No it's okay. I want to check it out. It should be me… she would hate someone invading her privacy."

Olivia input the code she'd remembered from the day before. Her heart wrenched when she saw hundreds of red notifications on each of Caro's apps—people reaching out to her who would never get a reply. Most were on an app Olivia didn't recognize. It was called Rush. When she clicked on it, she quickly realized that it had to be some kind of adult messaging service. It was set up like any social media app with messaging services and a feed of pictures and videos, but Olivia quickly moved on to the messages—the first image she saw was certainly not suitable for work.

The message inbox was filled to the brim. Every single message on there were from men. Olivia felt overwhelmed and disgusted as she scrolled through them, viewing only the previews. Each message was more lecherous than the last. Olivia had learned not to judge anyone's lifestyle, and she wanted to feel the same about Caro's choices, but she did feel uncomfortable at the way these men treated her—they didn't treat her as a human being. To them, she was little more than a piece of meat for them to feast on over and over until she was just bare bones.

She swallowed back her disgust and began to open the messages one by one. She didn't want to sit on the bed where Caro had once slept so she stayed standing, scrolling for long minutes at a time without finding much of interest. The messages Caro received were repetitive and unimaginative—almost as if the men had copied and pasted messages to her with the hopes of capturing her attention. From what Olivia could tell, Caro rarely replied. Sometimes she'd flirt with some of her regulars, people she knew in real life, perhaps. But the messages were playful, almost innocent given what had gone on. It didn't seem significant to the case, so Olivia kept going.

Two hours passed. Olivia's neck began to ache from hunching over the phone, but she didn't relent. She was sure that being thorough would pay off eventually. But it was difficult when Caro was clearly receiving hundreds of messages a day. After two hours, she had only made it through a week's worth of messages.

But then she found a message that made the searching worth it.

The message came from an account that had no profile picture. *CertifiedLover6284582.* A randomly generated name for the faceless man.

"Brock … come here and look at this message with me."

Brock was at her side in an instant, his hand steadying her as they read the message. Olivia's stomach churned in response to the words on the screen.

*CertifiedLover6284582: I don't have the courage to say this to your face, but I'm obsessed with you. I think about you every second of every day. At night, I take an image of you to bed with me. You just look so damn good. I shouldn't be risking everything to send you this message… you know me in person. But then again, I know you'll never guess who I am. Maybe that's part of the thrill of it. God, the things I would do to touch you. I don't think you'd ever let me though. Maybe someday.*

*CaromelKisses: Who is this?*

*CertifiedLover6284582: I bet you're dying to know.*

*CaromelKisses: Well, yeah, you've got my attention.*

*CertifiedLover6284582: And you've got mine. All the time.*

*CaromelKisses: This is weird. You do realize that?*

*CertifiedLover6284582: That's why I can't tell you who I really am. You'd be freaking out.*

*CaromelKisses: I already am a bit.*

*CertifiedLover6284582: It's good to know I'm on your mind… I know that's wrong but I just can't help myself. You're my drug.*

*CaromelKisses: If you know me at all, you know I don't want to be tied down. So you'll know I don't appreciate these kinds of messages. I don't want to be with you, whoever you are. So please, stop talking this way and move on. This isn't the flex you think it is.*

*CertifiedLover6284582: I want you. So so badly. I'd do anything. I'd kill myself if I thought I could spend five minutes in bed with you.*

*CaromelKisses: Please stop this.*

*CertifiedLover6284582: Would that I could.*

The messages ended there and Olivia was glad to close the conversation. Brock shook his head in disgust.

"Poor Caro. Who on earth is this creep? Do you think it's the same person who sent the letter?" Brock asked. "He claimed to know her in person too."

"I don't know… it's possible. But it feels different. The letter was confident… This feels more creepy. Like the person knows they're doing wrong and they're ashamed, but they keep going anyway. Maybe they were hoping that she'd guess it was them. It's definitely weird that this message was only sent a week ago. It's so recent."

"And now she's been hurt," Brock agreed. "And there's violence in those messages… seemingly only against himself, but if he's willing to do anything to himself, where do his boundaries stop? He's clearly unhinged."

"Are we assuming it's definitely a he?"

"You said there were no women on this app that you've seen, right? Seems like it. And Caro did seem to keep mostly male company. If he knows her in real life, then it's likely."

"Good point. Okay, so we're assuming this is a man. I'd rule out Anthony… he's already got a connection to Caro. By the sounds of it, she was keener on him than he was on her anyway. So who does that leave that we know of so far? Some of the staff here, maybe? Or Finn?"

"I can see Finn sending something like this… he has a creepy desperate air around him, and he doesn't seem to be deterred by rejection. But he's not really self-deprecating. He thinks a lot of himself. If you read back on the messages, this guy is talking about how she'd never go near him… Finn would never say something like that. He's too much of a narcissist."

"So that leaves us with… just about anyone. Great."

"Just a minute… we might be able to figure this out still," Brock said. "What about her personal texts outside this app? Conversations with her actual friends. We might be able to match up the tone of the texts from her friends and figure out who was messaging her. And the chances are you'll find some stuff there that's interesting anyway. We know everyone on this app is obsessed with her… what we need to know is who in her personal life toes the line."

"You're right. I should have been doing that from the start. What a waste of time…"

Brock squeezed her shoulder. "You haven't wasted a single second. This message could be key to the investigation. But now that we've got this as a lead, it will be useful to sort through her other messages. Take a screenshot of this message. We can come back to it easily that way."

Olivia felt glad to have Brock helping her out. She was perfectly capable of leading cases usually, but with everything she was feeling, it wasn't as easy to sort through the fog. Brock balanced her out and kept her in check, the same way she did for him when he was off his game. It was what made them such a perfect team.

Following Brock's sound advice, Olivia exited the Rush app and checked out Caro's messages. Again, she had left many messages unread. She began checking them out. Some of them were perfectly innocent, the kind of conversations Olivia had with her friends on a regular basis. Still, most of them were from men, and Olivia kept scanning them all, looking for similarities to the tone of the letter and the strange messages on the Rush app. She didn't find anything that seemed like a direct match just from first glance, despite being thorough.

It wasn't long before she came across messages between Caro and Anthony Berry. She lingered longer than she wanted to on the messages they shared, knowing that he still had plenty of reason to want Caro out of the way. Whatever had happened between them had messed up his life. That much was clear. And if his wife wanted to have Caro out of the way, then perhaps Anthony had indulged to keep her happy. The last messages they'd shared between them had certainly been frostier than usual.

**Anthony:** *Don't make this difficult. You knew it had to end at some point.*

**Caro:** *You promised me you'd handle this better. That nothing was going to stand between us.*

**Anthony:** *I never promised you anything, Caro. That's always been the issue. You wanted more from me than I was ever willing to offer.*

**Caro:** *I thought this meant something to us both. I know we never put a label on things…*

**Anthony:** *I'm married, Caro. That's my label.*

**Caro:** *So that's it? It's over?*

135

**Anthony:** *It was over before it began. It always had to be this way in the end. Just leave me the hell alone.*

Caro seemed to have some pride left over because she hadn't responded to the final message. Olivia checked the timestamps.

"These are dated shortly after Anthony's affair was exposed," Olivia pointed out. "It looks like Caro obliged and stayed out of his way."

"Good," Brock said, shaking his head. "She never should have gone there in the first place. Listen to him, acting like he shared none of the blame in what happened. It was his affair, not hers."

"Don't even. The more I think about him the more furious I feel," Olivia said, clicking out of their messages. "But it doesn't really help us. If she kept out of his way, in theory Anthony had no good reason to get back in touch or even to hurt her. Maybe we were wrong about how far he'd go to keep her out of the way."

"But what about his wife?" Brock pointed out. "She was the one with all of the fury, the one who got screwed over the most. Caro might have felt slighted, but at the end of the day, the wife was the one with the commitment to him. That's a motive to hurt Caro, don't you think? What if she enlisted Anthony to help? Make him pay it back for hurting her?"

"Sure, that sounds like a possibility. But we've never even spoken to his wife, we don't know much about her. We'd need some kind of lead."

"A lead like angry messages from an unknown number?" Brock said, peering over Olivia's shoulder and pointing something out. Olivia saw that he was right—there was an opened text box from an unsaved number, punctuated by aggressive words in the preview. Olivia clicked on the thread eagerly, scrolling back up to the start of the messages.

**Unknown:** *I know who you are and what you've done. I want you to stay the hell away from my husband. You might think you're clever because you tried to steal what's mine, but let me tell you, you're not. You're just a stupid whore with nothing better to do than become a homewrecker. I hope you'll learn your lesson from this mess because your troublemaking will lead you to bad places some day.*

*Caro:* I'm sorry you had to find out the way you did. But I wasn't trying to ruin anything. Anthony was never happy with you, and you can't possibly be happy with him. He should have the courage to end things with you so that you can both move on to better things. But since he hasn't done that, I think you should have some self-respect and leave him.

*Unknown:* Who the hell do you think you are? You think he loves you? Respects you? He told me that you meant nothing to him. Just a young, pretty thing for him to use and abuse. You're the one who should have some self-respect, throwing yourself at married men and posting naked pictures of yourself on the internet. Yeah, I know all about you and your type. You could have just stayed in your lane and said sorry, but you couldn't handle that, could you? Dumb cow. You'll get what's coming to you.

*Caro:* Bitter old hag.

*Unknown:* You've really crossed a line now. You'd better watch your back. Karma's coming for you.

"Well… that doesn't look good," Brock said. "Caro really wound her up there. And they mentioned Anthony. This must be the scorned wife."

Olivia nodded, her cheeks flushed. She felt almost embarrassed reading the conversation, seeing Caro lashing out at the woman whose marriage she had interrupted. It was a cruel side to her that Olivia hadn't seen, the side to her that Caitlin had told her about all along. Why did she have to start a fight with her? While Olivia was more than happy to lay the blame for the fallout of Anthony's marriage on Anthony himself, Caro was proving that it took the both of them to make it happen. She didn't seem to have any remorse, and that was the worst part of it. Olivia had been holding a candle to her this whole time, and it was hard to see this side of her. Was this the kind of thing Caitlin saw in her all the time?

"Don't overthink it, Olivia," Brock told her gently. "Not everyone is perfect all of the time. Caro clearly cared for Anthony more than he ever did for her. She was feeling hurt and defensive. It might not be a good look on her, but it doesn't mean it's her permanent state. She was a good person."

"Caitlin didn't seem to think so. Or Stephanie. Or Uncle Mark."

"They never even tried to like her. They saw she was different and pushed her away," Brock said gently. "I know this is tough. But you knew her. She wasn't a bad person. Just a flawed one, like the rest of us. You always looked up to her, so I guess you've been seeing her through rose tinted glasses. But she's just like the rest of us. Sometimes that can be hard to swallow."

Tears pricked at Olivia's eyes for a moment. She hated picking apart the woman she knew for the sake of being able to find who wanted her dead. It meant seeing all of the ugliest parts of her and her life. But Brock was right. She was still a good person. She'd known her long enough to know that about her. Olivia took a deep breath.

"What are we going to do about this? This woman was clearly angry with Caro. She even threatened her. That's pointing back toward Anthony too. Do we try to speak to her? Anthony wanted us to keep out of her way, that was for sure. What does she know that we don't?"

"We certainly need to find out. I say we go back over to their house. If we can speak to the wife alone, she might have a rational explanation for all of this… and maybe some insight into the affair that Anthony won't talk about."

"But what about Anthony? He made it clear we couldn't come back without a warrant. We could really land ourselves in trouble."

"We can call McCarty and take her with us. He can't stop us from trying to talk to his wife, even if he's not willing to talk to us. And at least with McCarty there we have some legitimacy for being there. We could stand to catch them off guard—we don't want to give them too much time to build a defense for our return. But it's up to you. I'll leave it in your hands."

Olivia took a deep breath. "Alright. We'll call McCarty. Let's get over there."

# CHAPTER TWENTY

OLIVIA FELT LIKE SHE WAS HOLDING HER BREATH THE whole way to Anthony Berry's home. She didn't know much about the woman he'd married—only that she had rightfully been angry when she discovered that he was having an affair. But otherwise, they'd been left in the dark entirely. Now, they'd have to try and talk to her. Olivia was almost certain that she wouldn't be feeling chatty, same as her husband. But the texts between her and Caro were too friction-filled to ignore. To say there was bad blood was an understatement. They needed to figure out just how deep it ran. Was Anthony's wife willing to kill in her fury? The scorned wife taking it out on the mistress? It was a story Olivia had heard many times before.

Olivia hoped they would find out.

As Anthony's house came into view, Olivia reminded herself to keep her cool. She couldn't allow for her newfound temper to get her into trouble again, even though it ran hot through her veins. Even if Anthony's wife was responsible for hurting Caro or they were both working in tandem, one wrong move could cost them the case, and maybe even her job. She couldn't afford to let this wreck her entire life. She'd lost so much lately, and her work was the only thing that kept her centered, other than Brock. After what happened to Jonathan, she had to fight for a reason to stay in the FBI, a reason to keep her life on track. If she couldn't manage that, she didn't know how she'd survive it all.

"McCarty said she's closing in on the property. She might be there as we pull up," Olivia said as Brock navigated up to the gates of Anthony's house. But Olivia frowned as she realized that the gates were wide open. "Huh…did she make it through already? Anthony's wife must have opened the gate for her…

"Or someone else got there first," Brock said. "We can't really slip in without an invite… we'll get caught for trespassing."

But Olivia was hardly listening. Because beyond the gate, on the pebble driveway, something had caught her eye. Two figures facing off with one another, their stances aggressive and almost primal. Olivia recognized one of them as Anthony, but the other was a woman. Perhaps his wife. There was no sign of Sheriff McCarty, and whatever was going on in the driveway seemed heated. Anthony's car was a few meters from where he stood, the door still open. He must have just returned from somewhere, only to be faced with some kind of faceoff.

"I don't like this," Olivia said. "I think she might be in trouble."

"I don't think so… it looks like he might be the one in trouble," Brock remarked as the woman advanced on him. Olivia watched in shock as the woman grabbed him by his shirt, shouting something unintelligible at him.

Then she drove her fist into his nose.

Olivia didn't even think before leaping out of the car. She couldn't stand by while someone was in danger, not even someone as loathsome as Anthony was. She ran through the gates and toward the fight, watching as Anthony went limp on the ground, the woman beating his face into a pulp. His head lolled to the side as he took blow after blow. The woman was in such a frenzy that she didn't even notice Olivia running at her.

Olivia threw herself at the woman, tackling her to the ground. Even as she did, she knew she would likely get in trouble for interfering, but she didn't care. Anthony groaned behind her and the woman thrashed beneath her, trying to lash out at her.

"Get the hell off me!" the woman cried. "What the hell are you doing on my property?"

"She's with me," McCarty said, jogging up behind them. "And we came here to investigate a murder. Imagine our shock to witness you beating up your husband. You must be Angela Berry."

"He's a lying, cheating, loathsome *snake*," Angela snapped, her wrists still pinned to the ground by Olivia. "What goes on in our home is none of your business."

"It became police business the moment you resorted to domestic violence. I'm sorry, but I have no choice other than to take you down to the station for questioning. You picked a bad day to get caught in the act… we have reason to believe you're connected to the murder, too. And your little display of violence has done nothing to help your case."

"Murder? What murder?" Angela snapped, foam gathering in the corner of her mouth like a rabid dog. She was still twitching, trying to escape Olivia's grasp, but Olivia held firm. She wasn't about to allow Angela to smash her face in too. Anthony seemed to be coming too behind her, Brock helping him to his feet.

"You too, Anthony. This has gone too far now," McCarty said. "Clearly there are things you haven't told us."

Anthony was breathing hard. He spat a glob of blood on the ground, anger burning in his eyes. "I told you, I'm not speaking to you until I have a lawyer."

"Well, find one fast, then. This isn't a game. A woman is dead, and clearly both of you have past grievances with the deceased. I don't need to tell you how this looks from our end. If you have nothing to hide, you have nothing to fear." McCarty paused, raising an eyebrow. "But the truth will out either way. You can be sure of that."

# CHAPTER
# TWENTY-ONE

OLIVIA AND BROCK FOLLOWED MCCARTY DOWN TO THE
local station, carting Anthony along while the sheriff
had Angela in the back of her car. The ride was in
complete silence. The drama of their fight had heightened
Olivia's senses and left her feeling on edge. It was a stark
reminder that nothing was ever as it seemed. Anyone was
capable of hurting anyone. And seeing Angela lashing out at
Anthony like some kind of wild animal was enough to make
her rethink everything she thought she knew.

All this time, they'd been looking at Anthony, assuming
he was the one with the capability to kill Caro. But now, it was
looking entirely possible that Angela had a motive—and the
violence needed—to kill her in cold blood.

At the station, Olivia and Brock waited while McCarty took the two of them into separate questioning rooms. It felt odd to be on the outside—they were used to being in the thick of it all—but Olivia was happy to be patient this time. It wasn't their case after all. They were lucky to be along for the ride at all.

After a while, McCarty came out to the waiting room and beckoned them back.

"I think you should be there while I question Angela," McCarty said. "I've given her a little time to cool off... she was in a bit of a state. But I think we can get her talking now."

"Has she said anything yet?"

McCarty shook her head. "Not so far. She's been so heated that I don't think she's thinking straight. Whatever caused her to launch herself at her husband, she must have been really aggravated. I'm hoping that she'll still be caught up in the moment and that she might slip up on what she says to us. If she does know anything about Caro's case, now is the time to find out."

Olivia nodded in agreement. She knew from experience that a wound-up killer was always more clumsy than a calm one. If she was involved in Caro's death, then she might show signs without even knowing it.

McCarty led the way and Olivia and Brock followed her inside the interrogation room. Angela's nostrils flared as she clocked Olivia's reappearance. After restraining her earlier in the day, Olivia clearly wasn't a welcome sight to her. Perhaps that was a good thing. If Olivia was setting Angela's nerves on edge, she'd be even more likely to slip up. And if she wasn't guilty, then she had nothing to fear. But Olivia could still see Angela's eyes, raged and seeing red as she punched her husband over and over again. That kind of violence didn't live inside everyone. Angela, knowingly or not, had just put a giant target on her back in this case.

"Let's start from the beginning, shall we, Angela?" McCarty said, sitting down opposite her and clasping her fingers together. "It's been a few weeks since you found out that your husband was having an affair with Caroline Knight... is that correct?"

Angela wavered, eyed Olivia briefly, then refocused her gaze on McCarty. "That's correct."

"And since then, your husband hasn't been in contact with her, is that also correct?"

"As far as I know. But he obviously can't be trusted," Angela said. McCarty cocked her head to the side.

"And why is that obvious?"

"Because he's a lying cheat. I thought that spoke for itself enough. I haven't trusted him for a long time. I always knew better than to let a man walk all over me. I stayed with him because I like my life for the most part. We have a nice house and I haven't had to work a day in my life. Can't argue with that, right? But when I signed up for marriage, I was naive enough to think that commitment would mean something to that scumbag. I never had proof, but I knew he was being unfaithful. Caroline was the first one I caught, but I'm sure there were others."

Angela rolled her eyes. She pointed at herself, her dyed blonde hair wild from the tousle outside her house and her mascara running. "I might not be much to look at now, but I'll tell you something... Anthony has a type. Caroline is me twenty years ago."

"Is that why you wanted to hurt her? Because she had everything you used to have?" Brock asked, raising an eyebrow. Angela's face softened.

"I didn't want to hurt her," Angela said. "I know it might not seem like I'm telling the truth after what you saw... but I've never hurt anyone in my entire life. Anthony has lied to me and hurt me so many times that I just... I erupted. I couldn't hold back my hatred anymore. And I regret it now. I shouldn't have lost control like that. I don't believe that violence solves anything. But I never saw Caroline again after the day I caught her with my husband."

"You spoke to her, though, didn't you?" Olivia said, holding up Caro's old phone. "We found texts between the two of you. She goaded you and you told her to watch her back."

Angela rolled her eyes. "Well, yeah. I didn't think I was asking for much from her. An apology would have been nice. But she was so full of herself. She didn't see the harm she was doing. Anthony probably told her I'm some old annoying shrew trying to ruin his fun. But she knew she was disrupting a marriage and she did it anyway. It was him I blamed, but she broke every code in the book. There's nothing cute or sexy about being a mistress, but she wore that as a badge of honor. She thought she loved him. Stupid girl. She was under his spell, just like I was." Angela's eyes turned sad and she shook her head. "How could I ever hate her for doing everything I did myself? I was her age once. I did everything I could to make Anthony mine. I've walked her path. I couldn't be angry with her for that. It would be hypocritical."

"So you're saying there was no bad blood between you?" McCarty asked.

"Look, I'm not saying I liked the girl. She was selfish and rude and willing to hurt anyone to get what she wanted. But I also think she was human. I was angry with her, but it's Anthony who I'm truly mad at."

"Let's go back to that then. Why did we arrive at your home to find you beating the hell out of him?"

Angela chewed the inside of her cheek. "I told you. I snapped. He's been lying to me again. He told me that he broke things off with that girl, and I believe he did. I was looking out for the signs of her... I came to recognize the smell of her perfume, the timings of his visits, the subtle changes in how he seemed when he'd been with her. It was like he wiped her off the face of the earth. I was sure it was all over. But he thought I was stupid, or crazy, or both. I started to smell other women's perfumes on him. Not just one or two, but multiple women. I guess he did like Caroline deep down... and when he could no longer have her, he replaced her with a horde of other women. I kept confronting him about it and he denied it. And he got away with it because then, I just didn't have any proof."

Angela smiled to herself, her grin almost sadistic. "But I had my ways of figuring him out. I tracked those women down, one by one. I spoke to each of them over the last week. Each of them promised they didn't know he was married... all of them young pretty things, of course. He won't settle for less now. And each one I spoke to told me things about him that I never wanted to hear... the disgusting, dirty things he wanted to do to them... he never wanted those things from me. Maybe he's become more perverted in his old age. Maybe he needs more to get his kicks... I wouldn't know. He hasn't so much as touched me in years. And when I considered the thought of touching him today... I thought about driving my fist into his smug face. Over and over again. Some sick fantasy I'd never considered before."

Angela scoffed. "Well. I figured if he's allowed to indulge then so am I. Why should he be the one who gets to have all of the fun? I decided I would give him one last chance to come clean. I met him at his car and asked where he'd been, who he had been seeing. I knew for a fact he'd been meeting one of his girls. But still he lied. So I just... let it all go."

The room was silent following her admission. Olivia considered what it must be like to be in her shoes—spending years being neglected and lied to, only to find out that there were multiple women standing in her place. Caro was just one of many, the first to be caught. Angela wasn't necessarily a monster, and if she was, it was one of her husband's own making. Olivia didn't condone what she had done at all. But the more she spoke, the more she felt certain that she wasn't looking at Caro's killer. If anything, she was looking at someone who could have killed Anthony earlier that day, had they not stepped in. She had reached her limit and become capable of hurt that she hadn't known was possible.

"I want you to know... I wasn't myself today. But Anthony has always been a devil in a thinly veiled disguise. If he and I go home together now, he won't have learned his lesson. He'll keep doing it over and over again. He'll drive me to new levels that I don't want to consider."

"You seem to have a very low opinion of him," Olivia said. "What I want to know... is do you think he would be capable of hurting Caro?"

Angela folded her arms around herself. "He's never hit me or anything like that... but he does have a temper. Sometimes he grabs me... hard. I have bruises up and down my arms from where he's tried to hold me still this week. I guess that only fueled my anger with him. Every time I'd accuse him of something— always something he'd actually done—he would grab me and shake me as if I was the one doing something wrong. So maybe he does have the impulse. I don't know. I guess I don't really know my husband at all. If I've learned anything recently, it's that."

"Where were you two nights ago?" Olivia asked her softly, though she didn't believe that Angela needed an alibi. Angela sniffed.

"Meeting one of his mistresses. We talked late into the night, drank some wine. I didn't get back until late. Anthony was home, asleep in the spare room. I don't know if he went anywhere while I was out. I didn't think to ask."

"Thank you," Olivia said with a nod. "For your honesty."

Angela sighed. "Am I still in trouble for what happened today?"

"I'm afraid so," McCarty said. "I'll hand you over to one of my officers. We still have a murder to solve."

Angela nodded. "Understood. For what it's worth... I hope you find and arrest whoever did it." She paused. "Even if it's my husband. That girl didn't deserve what happened to her."

"No," Olivia agreed. "She didn't."

# CHAPTER TWENTY-TWO

I T WAS LATE AFTERNOON WHEN OLIVIA AND BROCK FINALLY left the police station. After an unsuccessful second interview with Anthony (where he kept mentioning his non-existent lawyer through a bloodied nose) they had nothing else to do, but return to the cabin. Olivia was dreading it. Facing her family again after the accusations that had been thrown around wasn't going to be easy. There were clearly deep, unresolved issues among them all and she felt nauseous at the thought of confronting them. It was worse still considering that they had nothing to offer them. The day hadn't been completely unsuccessful, but they were no closer to figuring out who had killed Caro—they'd only ruled a couple of people out. And in the eyes of her family, what use would that be?

It was nostalgic in the worst kind of way. It reminded her of the long days and nights she had spent trying to solve the murder of her sister. Her family had never really understood how her job worked—it wasn't just going around rounding up bad people and putting them in prison within a day. Some cases took weeks, months, *years* to figure out. There were old cases left unresolved and put on the back burner that Olivia knew would haunt her for the rest of her days. But what else could they do? There wasn't always an answer. There wasn't always a trail of breadcrumbs to follow, or a simple solution to wrap everything up neatly with a bow. And yet if she returned to the cabin that night, only several days into the investigation, she'd open the door to expectant faces, all of them angry and confused by the way things had transpired so far. And Olivia would have to disappoint them all by telling them that she had no clue who would want to do this to Caro. Not to mention the fact that she still didn't entirely trust that her cousin and her boyfriend were in the clear.

Olivia didn't realize she had been gripping the seat until her hand began to cramp up. She slowly let go, flexing her fingers and trying to get a grip on herself. But even the strongest person could be felled by what she had faced the last few days. Past traumas were stacking up like dirty laundry in Olivia's mind, and it was all too much. She wasn't ready to end the day, to go back to judgment and anger. She breathed in through her nose.

"I don't think I'm ready to go back there yet," Olivia murmured to Brock. She was so quiet that she wasn't sure at first that he had heard her. But he slowly brought the car to a halt in a side street, killing the engine and turning to her.

"We don't have to go back there tonight if you don't want to. We can book a hotel if you'd prefer? Or we could just head back there late when everyone's in bed…"

Olivia sighed, reaching for his hand. "I don't think I can avoid it forever, as much as I might like to. They're still my family. But… we could stall a little? Maybe go somewhere for a while?"

Brock offered her one of his cheeky grins. They'd been few and far between as of late, and it was a welcome sight.

"If you wanted me to take you out for dinner, you could've just said so..."

"Alright, take me out for dinner."

"Where are your manners? The word is *please,* sweetheart."

*"Please, sweetheart."*

Brock's smile widened. "Your wish is my command. Where would you like to go?"

"Nothing fancy. I'd like to look at Caro's phone again for clues...there's still so much to search through, given that the Berry family were a bit of a bust... maybe we should just find a diner."

"You really know how to woo a man," Brock said with a wink. "One of these days we'll end up in a Michelin Star restaurant..."

"I doubt it. They're not likely to serve a burger and fries."

"Hey, I have levels. Don't put me in a box, Olivia. It's not right to stereotype."

Olivia smiled and shook her head as Brock started up the engine again. With everything that had been going on, it had been a while since she had truly appreciated being around Brock. Their time together was often tainted by some tragedy or another, or just used keeping busy. It was nice to be out and about with him, even if it was only to run away from her family for a while longer and to work on the case. Some of her best memories with him were of them running from their troubles, finding ways to make one another smile when the rest of the world seemed so bleak. It was a reminder that when they had one another, they had all they ever truly needed.

Brock managed to find them a diner in no time, though he didn't use his phone to direct them somewhere. Olivia chuckled to herself as they pulled into the parking lot.

"It's like you have a diner detector chip built in you..."

"And everyone should. How else are you supposed to find reliable grub wherever you might be?" Brock said. "I should invent a device for this exact purpose..."

"It's called the Maps app, Brock."

"No, this would be different. The map app shows you all sorts of boring things... road names, garages, hospitals...this would just be the good stuff. Diners only. The only navigation system we ever truly need."

"I'll remember that next time I have a broken leg and I need to find a hospital."

Brock tapped Olivia's forehead lightly. "Knock on wood. Don't jinx it, Olivia, your luck is bad enough as it is."

"Why are you touching my head when you say knock on wood?"

"Because you're thick as a plank," Brock teased, already dodging out of the way of Olivia's playful slap. They got out of the car together, playing around like a couple of teenagers as they made their way inside. And for a moment, Olivia managed to forget why they were there and how high the stakes were. Another thing she loved so much about Brock—he brought out the inner child she'd kept hidden for so long deep down inside her. He reminded her that there was still good in the world.

Inside the diner smelled of grease and salt. It made Olivia's stomach rumble. It wasn't often she actually craved that kind of food, but she realized she'd been running on empty for the last few days, barely stopping to eat. And now she felt ravenous. As they slid into a booth, she actually bothered to look at the menu, salivating at all of the greasy options on the menu. When a waitress came over to take their order, she felt like some kind of demon possessed her as she placed her order.

"Can I get the mozzarella sticks... a double bacon cheeseburger with peri peri fries... a strawberry milkshake... and a side of onion rings, please? Thank you."

The waitress gave her a strange look, but jotted down her order and then headed to the kitchens to place the order. Brock raised an eyebrow at her.

"Wow... feeling alright?"

"Yeah... just hungry, I guess."

"You're like one of those newly turned werewolves in films that can't stop eating once they become carnivores. Should I be worried about the next full moon?"

"Only if you're allergic to fur," Olivia replied with a glint in her eye. It gave her joy to see Brock burst out laughing. She made herself comfortable, pulling out Caro's phone. "I figured we might as well take our time and eat... we missed lunch today, and I'm in no hurry to go back. But I do think we need to look through Caro's phone again while we've got a few minutes."

"Yeah, don't let me stop you. Dig in ..."

Olivia began to check the phone again. A few new texts had arrived since she'd last checked the messages, most of them from casual friends who clearly had no idea what had happened. But Olivia was interested to see a message marked as from *Bestie* near the top of her inbox.

**Bestie:** *Are we still on for meeting up tomorrow? I didn't hear from you so I just wanted to check!*

Olivia chewed her lip. Whoever the person was clearly meant something to Caro if she'd marked them as 'Bestie' on her phone. Olivia racked her mind for a name, wondering if Caro had mentioned the person before, but nothing came to mind. Olivia wondered if Caitlin might know, but she doubted it. They hadn't been exactly on a friendly basis with one another, so it didn't make sense for Caro to talk about anything above surface level with her sister. She clicked on the message thread, wondering if she should say something to the person. They must not have heard about Caro yet.

When she scrolled back up the message chain, she saw that the conversation was unlike anything she'd seen in the other chats. Most of the people Caro spoke with had a flirtatious lilt to their tone, but this chat was very casual, never extending beyond friendliness. Somehow, it was jarring to read. When Olivia's food arrived, she picked at it, forgetting her hunger as she looked through the messages quietly. Olivia recalled the messages on the Rush app. How the person had claimed that Caro would never guess who they were. She hated that she was suspicious of the mystery best friend, especially given that she had no idea yet if they were a man or a woman, and they were the only person who seemed to treat Caro like a human being. But the messenger from Rush stuck with her as she read through messages commenting on new movies in theaters and sports scores. Was this person a likely candidate for a match to the Rush messenger? And if they were, was their obsession enough to fuel their urge to hurt Caro?

"You look worried. What did you find?" Brock asked Olivia. She gnawed absent-mindedly on a couple of sauce-stained fries.

"I'm just looking at her messages to her *bestie*… that's their name on her phone. And I'm just… suspicious. They seem perfectly nice, but maybe they're… too nice? Their messages stick out from everyone else's. They're not creepy at all."

"Ah. I see your conundrum. You're so used to seeing everyone else treating Caro like a piece of meat that it's weirder to see someone treating her like a human being."

"Right! This person sticks out like a sore thumb. And I feel guilty for not trusting their intentions at face value… but can you blame me? I don't really know who this person is or what they're about. At least the other people in her life present themselves as the vultures they are. And get this… they messaged her today, asking if they're still on for their plans. They don't appear to know what happened to her…"

"Either that or they think they're being smart by acting like they think she's alive. Solidifies their alibi if we come knocking," Brock said. He put his head in his hands. "Man, this job has turned us into such pessimists…"

"Maybe, but maybe not. We have to consider the avenue. I mean, if we look at the scope of most of Caro's relationships with people, there's a sexual element there somewhere. She wasn't shy about handing it out, and she made herself clear when she laid out her boundaries. If you were a guy…"

"*If* I were a guy?"

"Sorry. A sex-obsessed man who didn't already have a girlfriend, and you were best friends with Caro… would you start to wonder why she never picked you? Why she seemed to collect men like it was a hobby, but she never treated you the same way? Would you start to feel jealous?"

He considered it. "Well, no, not really? Like if we're friends then why would I cross that line with her? And besides, it's like you said—she didn't tend to discriminate. She was open to being with multiple men. As a guy, that would put me off, personally. I would want to be the one she chose or just stay friends."

"Okay, yes, but you're pretty standard in that respect. For a lot of guys, fighting for a chance with a woman like Caro is some kind of fantasy, right? And having known a lot of men... they bide their time. I've had *so* many friendships with guys go south because they eventually come out and say they want more."

"Which guys are we talking about here? Is that why you and Sam don't speak anymore?"

Olivia rolled her eyes. "Brock, we do speak, we're just busy people with lives. And no, he doesn't have a thing for me. You're getting off the subject."

"Sorry... curiosity got the better of me."

Olivia chewed her lip thoughtfully. "What if this person was waiting for an opportunity that never came? What if they felt rejected by the lack of interest and it made them feel low? Caro's stance is clear just by the name she put this person under... they were best friends, nothing more. And that must sting if you want something everyone else has, right? Most people would love to be called someone's best friend, but when you're relegated below all those men she spent time with... maybe it didn't mean quite as much. Maybe it just meant she found this person unappealing."

"Hm."

"In a sexual sense."

"Yeah, I got that, thanks. You could be right."

"I mean, just looking at some of these texts... whenever the subject of guys came up, this person was intent on telling Caro that none of them were good enough for her. I can't decide if that's just a girl being supportive of her best friend... or a guy hoping that she'll swear off other guys and run into his arms. Not that there's a hint of romance here between them. Caro never seems to flirt with this person. There's just zero hint of love at all here, at least in the romantic sense."

"But that's a point of interest... Was there anyone she ever rejected outright? Have you come across anything like that?"

"Not yet… but I didn't get through many messages in the scheme of things. Caro's phone must have been buzzing twenty-four seven."

"Maybe you don't need to read all of the messages to get to the point. Use the search box and type out some phrases that might work."

"Like what?"

He pushed her plate in front of her. "Here, you've barely touched your food. Eat while I do some experimenting. I'll see what I can come up with."

Olivia hesitated, but her stomach was still growling, so she passed the phone over to Brock and dug into her burger, suddenly ravenous. She relaxed a little, knowing she'd left the phone in capable hands, and enjoyed the rest of her meal. By the time she'd finished, her waistband was straining, but it felt good to be full, some energy returning to her body. And as she drank her milkshake to wash it all down, Brock's face lit up.

"Bingo," he said, sliding the phone over the table to Olivia. "Key phrase… *I love you.* This guy was clearly hoping to lock Caro down… you can imagine how that went down."

"Like a ton of bricks," Olivia murmured, scanning over the messages.

"And take a look at the contact name, too," he added.

Olivia's eyes shot up at the contact named *DO NOT ANSWER*, in all caps. Caro had clearly deleted the person's name from her contact list, but she hadn't bothered to delete the thread itself. Maybe she secretly liked having an admirer she could look back on. Perhaps Caitlin was right—Caro was a narcissist. Olivia shook off the thought—it didn't matter either way. They weren't there to figure out who she was as a person—they were there to get a read on her killer.

**DO NOT ANSWER:** *I love you, Caro. You must know that by now. I've never made it a secret.*

**Caro:** *I'm sorry, I don't feel the same. We've talked about this before.*

*DO NOT ANSWER: You've never even given me a shot. If you could just see me in a new light, if you gave me a chance to prove myself to you, I know you'd feel differently.*

**Caro:** *I don't think so, Nick. It's nothing to do with you. I'm not the kind to settle down. I don't want to fall in love. I thought we were friends.*

*DO NOT ANSWER: Of course we're friends. But there's more to it. I think you're kidding yourself. We spend all this time together… you're telling me you've never even considered it?*

**Caro:** *If I had, you'd know by now.*

*DO NOT ANSWER: I don't get you. Sleeping around like a whore, and you can't see the nice guy right in front of your eyes? I could give you everything you've ever wanted.*

**Caro:** *Says the man who just called me a whore. Maybe you're not as nice a guy as you think. And funny enough, I already have everything I want. That's why I don't need anything from you. Get over yourself.*

*DO NOT ANSWER: If you're going to be like this, I don't ever want to hear from you again.*

**Caro:** *Cya then.*

*DO NOT ANSWER: You've led me on.*

**Caro:** *I'm pretty sure I've done the opposite. I never once told you I liked you that way. You're supposed to be my friend. I can't believe you'd turn this all on its head this way and then blame me for not wanting it.*

*DO NOT ANSWER: Please, Caro.*

**Caro:** *I'm sorry. I can't give you what you want. End of discussion.*

Seemingly, it was the end of the discussion. Nick hadn't left a reply. Olivia looked up at Brock with her eyebrow raised.

"He fits the kind of profile we're looking for… but so do half the men out there. Then again, the rest of them still held a piece of her up until she died… Nick lost her completely. And this is dated from three months ago…"

"Enough time to stew in his rejection and plan a murder, you think?" Brock said. Olivia swallowed, anxiety squeezing at her chest.

"There's a way to find out where his head is at."

157

Brock frowned. "How?"

Olivia raised Caro's phone. "Let's give him a call."

# CHAPTER TWENTY-THREE

O LIVIA'S HANDS SHOOK A LITTLE AS SHE MADE THE VIDEO call, but she held the phone steady. She knew what she was doing was very much a risk. She was already wondering if it was a mistake to stick her nose in given that it wasn't her case, but McCarty had left her in charge of the phone, and she had to do something. Everyone was a suspect at this point, and they had to explore every possible avenue. If Nick had been rejected by Caro, it was entirely possible that he fit the profile of their killer—a jealous man wanting more than he could get.

Nick didn't answer the call right away, but when he did, Olivia could see that he was in bed. Light was streaming in through his window, so he clearly wasn't in the same state as them. He was a handsome blond, and very much shirtless in the video feed. He was rubbing his eyes as if he'd just woken up.

"Caro?" he said wearily, wiping more sleep from his eyes and sitting up in bed. "I wasn't expecting to hear from you again… sorry, I was crashing…" He blinked several times as his eyes adjusted. Then he realized it wasn't Caro looking back at him. He frowned, pulling the covers up over his naked chest. "Oh… this is Caro's phone number. Who are you?"

"I'm her cousin," Olivia said. "Olivia."

"Oh, hi! She's mentioned you a few times. What… What are you doing calling me from Caro's phone? Where is she?"

Olivia exchanged a quick glance with Brock over the table. "I guess I have a few things I need to speak to you about. But first… where are you?"

Nick ran a hand through his tousled hair. "Um… well, I moved to Australia about three months ago. I kinda had nothing to stay for… Caro and I had an argument and an opportunity came up with work so I just… Well, I left. And I haven't heard from Caro since so I figured I made the right decision. But I have to admit, I was excited when I thought she was calling."

"I bet," Olivia said tightly, though she was quickly realizing that she'd met a dead end. If Nick was living in Australia, then it seemed obvious that he had no idea about what had happened to Caro. He probably wouldn't even have had time to kill her and then get back to Australia. Which means that even with the texts they'd shared, he wasn't her killer.

"Can you, uh, maybe tell me what's going on? I feel kind of weird about this," Nick said sheepishly. Olivia took a deep breath.

"I'm sure Caro told you I'm with the FBI if she mentioned me?"

"Oh yeah, totally. She always thought you were pretty cool."

"Well… I'm sort of investigating something. She and I, we… We were away for a family vacation this weekend and… there's no easy way to say this. Caro was killed."

Nick's smile dropped. "What?"

"She was… murdered. I'm unofficially helping with the investigation and… well, I'm looking into every avenue. I'm sorry to be the one to give you the bad news."

Nick's eyes filled with tears and he swallowed. "Wow, I... I don't know what to say. I... I'm really going to miss her. We had our differences but I cared about her. Very deeply."

"I know. That's sort of why I was calling. I'm looking through her phone, trying to figure out who would want to do this and why. It's what we call a crime of passion... we think whoever did this pre-planned it and did it out of some kind of love or hate. It's just a case of figuring out which it is."

"And you thought... based on how Caro and I ended..."

"We have to look into every avenue..."

Nick shook his head, holding up a hand. "No, I understand. I know that it must have looked bad on my end. I was head over heels for her... or at least, I felt like I was. I guess since I've moved away, I've had a little clarity. The thing about Caro is that she... she had this effect. No one really escaped it. And given her, um... lifestyle, I guess if you weren't in on it, it made you feel like you were somehow... missing out? Inferior? I thought I wasn't good enough for her and that's why I couldn't lock her down. But I realized that she was right. She just never wanted that. She was looking for a friend and I blew it just because I couldn't keep my thoughts straight. And I never got the courage to call her and tell her I was sorry..."

Olivia didn't want to mention that Caro had all but deleted him from her life the moment their messaging ended, so she kept her mouth shut. She didn't want to lie to Nick either. He sniffed mournfully.

"Damn... I wasn't expecting a call like this this morning. I just wish I could have spoken to her one last time. Maybe we could've made up and been friends... I'm seeing someone else now and I feel like we could've moved on from that whole mess... but I'm too late."

"I'm so sorry. I know this must be hard to hear."

"Not half," Nick said, shaking his head and rubbing his neck. "Honestly, I'd like to be alone right now if you think we can leave this here..."

"Actually... I was hoping that you might have some insight for me," Olivia said quickly. "I know it's not what you want to think about right now, but it might help me figure out what happened to Caro. Do you think you can spare a few more minutes to talk about her?"

Nick wavered for a moment and then nodded. "Sure… for Caro. I'd do anything to help her."

"I know she'd be so glad to hear that, Nick. I just want to ask a few questions about the people she… liaised with. I've only just become aware of… well, her lifestyle and the men she interacted with. I'm searching for answers, but there are literally hundreds of people on her phone messaging her. But there have been a few instances where people have sent her super creepy messages and threats."

Nick shook his head. "I hate to say it, but it doesn't surprise me. I know how she made me feel as a normal guy. I can imagine that she inspired extremism in a lot of guys. They'd do anything for her. It was almost like a cult. These guys just treated her as though she was their goddess. I guess we all saw her in some kind of angelic light…"

Olivia fought the urge to wrinkle her nose at the sentiment. She wasn't so sure that Nick's obsession truly was over, but he wasn't a candidate anymore. He couldn't be based on his location. That's why she needed to glean as much information from him as she could.

"Did you know any of these men personally? And would you expect any of them to be… creepy, for lack of a better word? She received messages on an app called Rush from a man who claimed to be someone she knew in real life. He said she'd never guess who he was… but he was obsessed with her. He was saying all these sleazy things to her, but he also thought she'd never give him a chance."

Nick's mouth twisted in an uncomfortable smile. "You thought that guy was me until five minutes ago, didn't you? Based on the messages she and I shared?"

Olivia shifted in discomfort. "Not necessarily. It was a possibility we entertained, yes. But I can see now that you couldn't have been the killer. Your location alone is a pretty solid alibi."

"It's okay... I get it. The way I was back then, I would've done pretty much anything to get what I wanted. That's when I started to realize that it was an unhealthy obsession. I'm not even sure it can be called love. And as much as a lot of the guys in her life thought they loved her, I'm not sure any of them ever did. She never let anyone in close enough to love her that way. But there were definitely a few of the guys that kind of fit what you might be looking for... I mean first off, there was Anthony Berry. He was the only one she was ever really besotted with, I imagine. I think it was because he acted disinterested and it kept her on her toes. But if he was so unbothered, explain to me why he was with her every single week, like clockwork? No one else had that much of her attention. She definitely had favorites... a few of the guys at the hotel were on her radar, maybe because they were under the same roof. But if you asked me who her top guy was, it was Anthony."

"I've already spoken with him a few times. He's a piece of work."

"I never met him properly, but anyone in Caro's circles hated him. We were jealous, of course, but there was more to it. It was the fact he had a wife that rubbed us all the wrong way. Most of the guys wouldn't dream of seeing someone else if they had Caro, even if she was seeing a hundred other guys. It's like I said... it was like she had us under a spell. So yeah, Anthony rubbed us all up the wrong way. It was weird too... he was obviously an older guy so I guess we wondered what he had that we didn't."

"Do you think he'd hurt her?"

"I honestly couldn't say. I didn't know him well enough. But I get the feeling he had a dark side to him. He gives off a vibe... kind of aggressive, possessive, an alpha male. And his indifference... maybe that was more of a lack of feeling anything at all. Kind of psychopathic, you know?"

Olivia didn't often appreciate the people she interviewed trying to put labels on suspects in this way, but she had to admit, Anthony did fit the bill of a psychopath in some ways. He clearly didn't care about anyone other than himself to the point of cruelty, and he'd manipulated, lied and cheated his way into Caro's life. He was completely lacking empathy and he didn't seem to care what people thought of that. But he had charm, that was for sure. Or else why would Caro be so drawn to him?

"Was there anyone else of interest?" Olivia asked. "We have been reading through some messages, trying to look for the most unlikely people…the sorts of people Caro wouldn't suspect of being interested in her. We wanted to match the person to the message on Rush. So we're looking for someone she isn't romantically involved in… but someone who likely had unrequited feelings for her."

"Well, I can tell you who that would be right away. Does the name Nathan Calloway ring a bell with you?"

Olivia frowned. "I haven't seen that name pop up on Caroline's phone… would you describe him as her best friend? There was a message chain under the name *Bestie* that we thought might fit the bill."

"Possibly. They've been good friends for quite a while, and he was always around. He definitely wasn't Caro's type… I don't like to say that she was out of his league, but if we're being honest… he was leagues below. I met him a few times and I didn't much like him. It was always hard meeting her friends, knowing that they were usually sleeping with her, getting exactly what I was hoping for… but Nathan was different. I know she never touched him. And she couldn't see it, but he hated any guy in her life. *Hated.* I mean, I wasn't even one of her guys and he would look at me like he wanted me dead. No word of a life. He was truly obsessed, but she never saw it. He was just waiting for a time to strike. He's one of those 'nice guys'… he thought he deserved her time because he was polite to her and treated her with respect."

Olivia raised her eyebrow. She didn't want to point out that Nick had also referred to himself as a 'nice guy' to Caro to try and win her over. But she saw his point. He was always there, on the back burner, waiting to be chosen. Hoping she would turn around and see that he'd always been there from the start, always been good to her, always given her time and energy and praise. But Olivia knew well enough that love didn't work that way. Nathan could wait forever and never have her.

And maybe he realized that.

"Bear with me a moment, Nick ..."

Olivia minimized the call and went into Caro's call log. Why had it only occurred to her now to question who Caroline had been speaking to on the night of her death? She was half expecting it to be Nathan under the title of Bestie. But her heart sank when she saw who her last call had been to.

An unanswered call to Caitlin.

Olivia swallowed. The call was made around midnight. Why had she felt the need to call her sister so late? Why had she reached out to the one person who had never given her the love she wanted? It was hard to see it before her, plain as day. But it also gave her more questions than answers. She scrolled down through the calls, looking at who she had spoken to after she'd wandered out into the forest. She'd made a few calls to various people. She'd even tried Anthony, but he hadn't picked up the call. But the other names weren't familiar to Olivia, and she wondered whether that was significant or not. Had she just been reaching out to anyone who would answer at the drop of a hat? Was she just looking for some familiar human connection? After an evening with her family, that seemed like it made sense. After all, she never felt like she belonged there. Maybe it was the only way she knew how to make herself feel good.

But neither Nathan nor *Bestie* appeared on the call list. Still, Olivia was beginning to feel suspicious of the man Nick had mentioned. Sure, he was likely biased, but he could have picked out any one of Caro's posse to hone in on. It was Nathan who had immediately come to mind when Olivia had detailed their profile. That had to mean something.

She opened up the call again and took a deep breath.

"Sorry, I just wanted to follow up on something there. Thank you for all of your help. Are there any other names you'd suggest that we follow up on before I let you go?"

Nick chewed his lip. "Honestly? Not really. If you'd asked me for a list of men who crossed lines with Caro, I could give you more. But you said you were looking for someone that she'd never been romantically involved with. And he never, ever stood a chance. I can say for certain that it must have played on his mind.

Whether he'd hurt her for never choosing him…I couldn't say. But I think it's a good place to start. Maybe…maybe if I think of anything else, I could call back?"

"That would be great. Thank you for your help, Nick. I'm sorry again to be the bearer of bad news."

"Thank you for letting me know," Nick said with a sad smile. "The world won't be the same without her."

# CHAPTER
# TWENTY-FOUR

THERE WAS NO CHANCE OLIVIA WAS HEADING BACK TO the cabin anytime soon. She asked the waitress to bring her and Brock some coffee and began her search online for Nathan Calloway. If Nick had pointed them in the right direction, she knew she might be about to look into the face of Caro's killer.

It wasn't difficult to find him, given that she had access to Caro's phone and social media. A quick search of her socials brought up a lot of information of interest. Brock slid into the booth beside Olivia to get a better look at what was going on.

"Nick wasn't lying... this guy is leagues below Caro," Olivia commented as she scrolled through Nathan's photos. He was a pudgy man around her age with a wispy, patchy beard. His thick dark hair was styled with too much gel and flecked with dandruff in every picture, and his clothes fit him poorly. He had a closed-mouth smile and bright eyes that made Olivia feel uncomfortable to look at. Nothing about him was very appealing.

Yet he always seemed to be surrounded by women in photographs. As Olivia scrolled through, she saw that Caro often featured in his photos, including every single one of his profile pictures. It made them look like a couple, his arm always around her. She was grinning in every picture, looking carefree. Was it possible she had missed the monster beside her?

"What's with all the girls on his arm?" Brock mused as they looked at more and more photographs. All of the girls that tagged him seemed to refer to him as their best friend, or the sweetest guy they knew. Olivia chewed the inside of her cheek.

"I have a theory."

"Go on."

"It's not very nice."

"You can say it."

Olivia sighed. "If I was one of those women, hanging around with a guy like him… it's probably because they feel safe around him. Because they never consider him an option, so there's no danger of blurred lines. And they assume he knows that too."

"Wow. That's rough for him."

"I know, it sounds awful now that I say it out loud. But every single one of these girls is beautiful… they have the pick of the lot. There's a reason they're constantly referring to him as 'bestie' or 'sweetheart.' They're making it clear for the world to see that he's not their type. I mean, maybe he's their safety option…"

"Safety option?"

"You know… the nice, means-no-harm guy that you might date if you run out of options… because at least he'd treat you well? I'm just theorizing here…"

"Does every woman have a friend like that?"

"No, of course not! It's mean and shallow and offensive to the guy… but it does happen from time to time."

"Please tell me I wasn't your safety option."

"Oh, please. You spend every hour of every day winding me up and you're too good looking for your own good. You know you're everyone's first choice."

He grinned. "Well, that's my ego stroked. Good to know. But you think Caro might have felt that way about him?"

"Hmm… I don't know. Caro was particularly spoiled for choice. And if Nathan really is the guy she labeled as 'bestie' then it seemed like they really did have a friendship. They would banter with one another and talk every single day. She obviously felt that she could trust him. But I can't shake off what Nick said about him… that he treated guys differently to how he treated her, and that he hated any guy that wasn't him. It sounds like he was capable of anger to another level. I mean, if we're comparing the two… neither of them were romantically involved with her, and both were her solid friends. But Nick is handsome and clearly has a good heart, deep down. Nathan, on the other hand? Perhaps the polar opposite. Based on Nick's account, at least."

"Which is likely biased."

"Sure. But it's interesting to consider. Do you see a single guy in any of these pictures? He's wearing these girls like a trophy on his arm. And then there's Caro. The grand prize in his eyes. Imagine how it would make him feel to see her pick anyone, but him. He would've hated that if he was actually obsessed with her. And it would explain why he hated Nick. But he would've worn any title Caro gave him like a badge of honor. Maybe he just decided he needed more…"

"And if he couldn't have her, then no one could."

Olivia nodded mournfully. "Exactly."

"So what now?"

"Well… I guess we should try and track him down to talk to him. We could call by his work, he's tagged it on his profile… Dusty's bar. That's not far from here. Caro used to work there for quite a while. I visited her there a few times when she was on shift. She said the tips were insane."

"I bet they were," Brock said, rolling his eyes. "And it makes sense that they could've met through work. They were spending a lot of time together, so that would've made them closer. Or else they might not have found much reason to keep hanging out."

"Well, I suppose it's a testament to his character that she kept on speaking to him once she found her new lifestyle. She obviously saw him as a good guy. We're probably being harsh… but we need to speak to him either way. If he's her best friend then he'll have insight that we don't. Assuming he's not the one that killed her."

"He messaged earlier, didn't he? Asking if they were still meeting up tomorrow?"

"Yeah, but it's possible that he's misdirecting us. He could be aware that the police are looking at Caro's phone for evidence. So he's pretending he doesn't know she's dead in order to make him seem innocent. He might even be relying on it for an alibi. But it's not strong enough for us to discount him."

Brock finished up his coffee. "I guess we should settle the bill and head over there then. I'll message McCarty and keep her updated. We should be keeping her in the loop."

"Yeah, definitely. But let's play this cool. We don't need to play our hand. He likely won't know who we are when we show up. Let's see if we can get a read on him before we start digging for information from him."

"Agreed. Lead the way, babe."

They left the diner five minutes later and Olivia directed Brock to the bar. It had been a long time since she'd last been there, but by the looks of it, it hadn't changed much. It was a bit of a dive with a broken neon sign and ripped leather booths. But it had Caro written all over it. From the moment they entered the bar, it had a wild vibe to it, with drunken men wandering around and shouting over one another to be heard. There was some sports game on the TV in the corner that had a bunch of them up in arms, and the bar was crowded. Olivia was one of three women in the entire joint, but most of the bar staff were women, and pretty ones at that. Olivia thought Nathan would be easy to spot among them, but she couldn't see his face.

She sidled up to the bar with Brock a few paces behind her. Seeing that she was a woman, the men parted for her. She could tell she was being stared at which made her blush. Unlike Caro, it wasn't her dream to be perceived by every man she came across. She preferred to blend into the background. Especially from a work perspective. She stuck out like a sore thumb there at the bar, and it wasn't going to be easy to go unnoticed if Nathan did show up.

But as a sour-faced bartender served her, she had come to the conclusion that he wasn't there. She decided to switch tactics.

"I'm actually here to visit an old friend," she said with a smile. "Is Nathan working tonight? I thought he'd be around ..."

The woman frowned. "He *should* be here. He's on the schedule. But I'm spending my day off behind a smelly bar because he didn't bother to show his face. That's three days in a row now."

Olivia raised her eyebrow. *I wonder why.* "Oh, really?"

"No one has so much as heard from him. It's not like him to let us down, but that's men for you. Can't trust them one bit."

"Huh ... you said he hasn't shown up in *three days?*"

"Yep. Look, are you ordering a drink? I don't need these boys hollering any more than they already are."

"Okay, sorry. I guess if Nathan's not around, I don't need to stay ..."

Olivia edged away from the bar and Brock frowned as she headed straight for the door again, rushing out into the cold evening air.

"What happened?"

"It's got to be him," Olivia said, her heart racing. "He hasn't shown up for work in three whole days. Apparently he's always punctual and has a perfect record, so what reason does he have to skip out on work and go no contact? Because he killed her. He killed her and then regretted it, most likely. Maybe he's already left town ..."

"But the text ..."

"He was smart enough to think to send a fake text, but not to think we'd check out his workplace. He probably assumed he had much more time to play with ... after all, we've had plenty of leads to look into. He must have been counting on that, or maybe he thought the police wouldn't be able to keep up."

ELLE GRAY | K.S. GRAY

"And the hammer?"

"We assumed it was some kind of tool relating to the killer's profession... but everyone has tools around the house. A hammer isn't unusual. I think it's likely just something he thought would do the job. But now it all makes sense to me. The box at the bottom of the tree where he hid the weapon... who would Caro tell about her dearest childhood memories? Her best friend. Who would know to find her at the tree and the lake house? Her best friend."

"What's your theory?"

"I think he went to see her. I think he wanted to try and confess his feelings to her... but he had a failsafe if she rejected him. To kill her. Because he thought he loved her more than anyone else possibly could. And if he couldn't have her, no one else deserved her. It just makes so much sense to me... I'm sure it's him."

"Okay, let's not jump the gun. We need evidence to back us up. And if he's really gone off the radar, then the best place to start is at his house. We're going to need McCarty in on this. We can't just go to his house. Where would we even..."

"I'll call McCarty. She can run his records," Olivia said.

"Good thinking. I'll do an online search."

It only took a few minutes for them to find the address, thanks to McCarty's quick search of driver's license records. McCarty promised to meet them there, and soon enough, they were back on the road. It was a bittersweet feeling for Olivia—she always felt anticipation when they were closing in on their suspect, but this time was different. She was invested in the outcome in a different way this time. She wanted justice for her cousin and she wanted the person who hurt her to be put away for life. If they had the right guy, and she felt sure that they did this time, she would be able to put the case to rest. But she'd never forget what had happened. She'd never forget that someone decided to snuff out her beautiful cousin's light. All this pain and suffering, for what? Who had won here? Not her, or her family, or Caro. And certainly not Nathan.

His address led to an apartment complex on the edge of town. It was the kind of place you'd expect a young man working night shifts at a bar to live—small and unassuming. But Olivia felt a presence about the place. Like it held the key to what they were looking for.

McCarty arrived a few minutes after they pulled up outside the place. They met her with grim handshakes and she looked stern as she pulled her gun from her holster.

"This definitely seems promising," McCarty agreed following Olivia's catchup for her. "We can see if he's home… but if not, I say we go in."

"We don't have a warrant," Brock said.

"We'll get one called in. In the meantime, I trust your judgment here. But I'll need to go in first."

"Understood," Olivia said with a nod. It made sense—she wasn't armed and she didn't want to interfere with McCarty's case. McCarty nodded firmly and ushered them to follow her. She tried the call box for Nathan's apartment, but none of them were surprised when no one answered. Luckily, someone was exiting the building, so they slipped inside while the door was open.

Olivia's heart was in her throat as they crept up to the third floor. The whole place smelled like cigarette smoke, and there was a buzz of a party taking place down the hallway. But apartment 47 was quiet as a mouse. McCarty hesitated outside the door for a moment before banging her fist on the door.

"Nathan Calloway? This is the police. Open up!"

There was no reply from inside. Olivia sniffed the air and noticed that there was a slight rotting smell coming from inside. She dreaded to think what it was or what it meant. All she knew was that they needed to get inside.

McCarty didn't need to be told. After knocking again to no response, she began to batter the door with her shoulder. When the first few tries were unsuccessful, Brock stepped forward to help, butting the door with such force that the door burst right open on the first try.

McCarty rushed into the room, gun at the ready. But the room was dead silent. Olivia followed her inside, her nose wrinkled against the smell. The apartment was a mess— there was rotting food in the trash, unwashed plates by the sink, and dirty clothes scattered throughout the living area. While McCarty checked the bathroom and bedroom, Olivia and Brock stayed back, surveying the room in silence. It was a horrible apartment, but nothing they hadn't seen before.

McCarty came out of the bedroom, looking pale. She swallowed.

"There's no one here," she said hoarsely. "But you should come and see this."

Olivia's heart squeezed as she followed McCarty into the bedroom. When she saw the walls, she felt her stomach twist with nausea.

On every inch of the walls, Nathan had plastered images of Caro. Some were photographs of the pair of them together, but most of the pictures were snapshots of her alone. Not necessarily ones taken by him either. He'd clearly found pictures wherever he could and printed them off.

And then there were the explicit images. Screenshots from her explicit videos, shamelessly tacked to the wall like some kind of pornographic museum. When Olivia looked up at the ceiling, she saw that it too was covered in pictures of her. She pictured Nathan lying on the grubby bed, looking at those photographs and fantasizing about her. Her throat closed over and she choked out a sob. She had seen worse before—it was part of the job—but to think someone had obsessed over her own cousin this way was too disturbing. It made the reality of it all hit home. There was no question about it now.

Nathan had killed Caro.

"I'm sorry... but there's more," McCarty said. She opened the bedside table and ushered Olivia over to look inside. Her legs felt numb as she walked over, trying not to stumble over her unsteady feet. She didn't want to look inside, but she knew she had to. There were answers there that she needed to discover.

The drawer was full of death.

# CHAPTER TWENTY-FIVE

OLIVIA TREMBLED AS SHE LOOKED INSIDE THE DRAWER. There were hundreds of polaroids scattered in the drawer, among other little trinkets that she couldn't quite process yet. She didn't have the strength to look properly when she saw what was before her.

Because each of the polaroids was of a dead woman.

Right on top of the pile was Caro. The picture showed her lying where they'd found her in the forest, her eyes unblinking, her skull caved in and caked with blood. Her beauty remained, but there was nothing left of the person she had been, nothing in those eyes. Olivia fought back tears as she fetched a glove from her pocket so as not to contaminate the evidence. This was everything they'd need to take Nathan down if they could catch him, but it didn't feel like a victory. Not when Olivia could barely process the fact that a photo of Caro's body lay atop so many others. Women Olivia had never seen before, but women she felt the loss of all the same. Because they'd all been like Caro once. Full of life and love and a little bit of wildness. Now they were reduced down to bodies lying alone in the dark. Women who died because a man claimed to love them. How could that ever be love?

"Are you alright?" McCarty asked gently, touching Olivia's elbow with care. Olivia nodded, but of course she wasn't. But she didn't have the luxury of time to sit with her feelings. She continued to look through the photographs, sifting through them with trembling fingers. There were multiple shots of the same people, including Caro. Olivia counted at least four others, though the quality of some of the pictures was bad, and some of the photographs were beginning to fade. And then there were others as she got deeper into the pile. So many bodies that Olivia was losing count of the dead sets of eyes looking up at her from each photograph. She felt sick, but she kept going. Stopping now would be a disservice to them all.

Right at the base of the drawer was a picture of a younger woman, possibly aged fifteen or sixteen. Her photograph seemed the oldest, her clothes dating back to the early 2000's. She looked very much the child she was, but all her youth had been sucked out of her when she'd died. There was a vicious wound on her cheek, enough so that the bone had caved in on her face. But it was the wound to her head that had clearly been the killing blow. Olivia swallowed.

"I think this was his first kill," Olivia breathed. "I saw an old photograph of her on Nathan's social media. A post about her going missing when they were kids. The caption...the caption said he still thinks of her every day. That he missed her all the time. He would've been sixteen at the time."

"God, he's sick," McCarty said, anger in her voice. "Who could do this?"

"And how did he get away with it? To kill someone at age sixteen... and to keep lying about it... this tirade has been going on for half of his life. He just kept going. And no one had any idea of what he was capable of."

"He must have some kind of charm to not be connected to any of these cases… or he's pretty good at hiding. Though what we are seeing here doesn't really point to that at all, does it?"

"Maybe this time was different for him. I mean, look at this place. Caro has taken over the entire room. And from what we know, he's been in her life for some time. I guess maybe he was willing to hold out the longest for her."

Olivia's hand brushed over some of the other objects in the drawer. A plastic figurine of a ballerina. A wad of old concert and cinema tickets. A pair of used underwear. A hair tie. A lone stick of gum in an old packet. A broken watch. A lanyard with keys attached. An empty bag of chips. A tissue streaked with mascara stains.

"Trophies?" Brock asked gently. Olivia frowned.

"Yeah…but more than that. A collection. Like a scrapbook of memories…he started collecting these long before he killed these women. I think they started out as things he kept because he was infatuated. Like the tissue… I'm picturing some scenario where he comforted one of them and felt like a hero for mopping up her tears. So he kept it. And the underwear… perhaps one of them gave in to him before the rejection that got them killed. I guess when things didn't go his way… he'd finish up with them. Like a defense mechanism, almost."

Olivia's hands shook with anger as she shut the drawer. "They couldn't reject him if they were dead. And once he'd killed them… they were vulnerable to be photographed by him. So he could always remember them the way they were, or the way he wanted to perceive them. Like they really were lost lovers and not just women not interested in him. That's my assumption. He arranged them to look a certain way…provocative, almost. Glassy-eyed because of lust, not because they were dead. He put thought into the photographs. He wanted them to be a legacy of a memory that never came to fruition. If he couldn't have them in life… I guess this is how he got his kicks."

"Then why would he leave all of this behind?" McCarty murmured. "He's spent all of this time curating his collection... he's even added to it recently. Literally just a few days ago when Caro was killed. But now there's no sign of him, and he's obviously been gone for at least a few days. So why didn't he take his collection with him?"

Olivia shook her head, swallowing back her pain and anger.

"He must have been aware that he needed to make a quick getaway. It's only been a few days since he killed her... something likely spooked him enough to leave everything behind. Or maybe something was different about it this time around and he was running away from what he'd done."

"What do you mean by that?"

Olivia exhaled slowly, reopening the drawer of horrors. She took a deep breath, her gloved hand brushing through the polaroids.

"Like maybe he cared more this time around. He's been in Caro's life for a while. These other women... It was almost like a hit and run. The dates on these photographs... The last one was a good five years ago. That must be when he moved here... or at least when he started working at the same bar as Caro. Maybe he thought he could change. That she would be the one who would stick. He was patient, willing to bide his time. But he must have reached the final straw the other day and killed her. Maybe some part of him didn't want to do it. Maybe he's lost his mind and forgot how to be careful." Olivia shook her head to herself. "It doesn't matter. It's him. It's always been him. All these women... dead for no reason. Dead because they didn't want to entertain a lonely man."

"Olivia..."

"I'm fine, Brock!" Olivia snapped. Then she immediately regretted it. She turned to Brock. "I'm sorry. I didn't mean..."

"Hey, it's okay," he said gently, cupping her cheek. "I think we need to get you out of this room. Let's get you some air and I'll call for backup. Sheriff, I presume you'll need to get a team out here?"

"I think that's necessary," she agreed. "We need someone looking out in case he happens to come back. And maybe we can try to piece together where he might have gone."

"On it," Brock said, gently guiding Olivia from the room. She hated the idea that she couldn't handle this like any other case, but after all of the things she'd seen and dealt with, she knew she had to cut herself some slack. No one could see those things related to someone they loved and come out unscathed.

Brock shut the door to the bedroom and clutched Olivia's shoulders, his eyes kind and loving.

"I'll be okay," Olivia began to insist, but Brock shook his head.

"You don't need to convince me of that. You're the strongest woman I know. You're allowed to be hurt. You're allowed to be angry."

Olivia took a deep breath, feeling validated by his gentle affirmations. She nodded in agreement. He was right. She didn't need to make excuses for her own humanity. Not when they were dealing with a monster.

"We need to find him. We have to make it happen."

"We will. We always do," Brock said, pulling her close to his chest and kissing the top of her head. It was impossible for Olivia to let go of the anxiety that had taken hold in her chest, but she took a few deep breaths and clutched Brock. It was enough to keep her going. She pulled away from him, feeling a little of her strength returning.

"Make the calls. I'm going back in there."

"Are you sure?"

"Yeah. The sooner we find what we're looking for, the sooner we can pin everything on him and get this over with. Then we can grieve."

"Alright. But take care of yourself in there, okay? Know your limits."

Olivia offered him a slight smile, recognizing his efforts to therapize her. But it kind of worked. She was grateful that Brock found a way to talk his feelings out with his therapist, but even more glad that he taught her to manage her own in return. *Money well spent,* Olivia thought to herself.

Olivia took a deep breath and headed back into the hellhole that was Nathan's bedroom. McCarty looked up as she entered, holding up a black notebook. It was well used, the pages fanned out and almost fluffed up between the two covers.

"A journal, I think. Although some of the pages don't even make much sense. Here, I want to know your thoughts."

A little reluctantly, Olivia took the notebook. She hated the fact that the pages were grubby with use. Olivia imagined the obsessive man, pawing through the pages whenever he was fantasizing about killing or his current obsession. Olivia flicked through some of the pages, the writing sometimes neat, and other times an almost illegible scrawl. It was like an indicator of the mood he was in; either calm and collected or utterly wild, driven by lust and adrenaline.

The pages at the start of the book weren't related to Caro. They talked of other women, a few pages dedicated to each of them. They must have been the other victims. While he never mentioned killing any of them in the pages, there was always some vague yet dark utterance before their presence in the diary disappeared entirely. *Gemma has to go away soon... Delilah has lost her way, we can't continue this way... I have to see Anne-Marie one final time...*

There was one name that didn't seem to have a tragic ending. There were two separate mentions of a woman named Tanya. The first time she was mentioned, it almost seemed as if Nathan hadn't been that interested in her, and then the entries blurred into mentions of Gemma. The second time she was mentioned, Tanya's reappearance still didn't seem to stir Nathan the way the others had. Or rather, he didn't have the same response to her as he did the others.

*I'll always be at home with Tanya. She loves me. I could love her, if I chose to. But I want more in my life than love. And if I choose to love her back, it can only end well. I'm not sure that's what I want.*

*Interesting,* Olivia thought. It sounded like Nathan was more interested in women who weren't likely to want him back. Perhaps it was because he had high standards, impossible ones even. He liked the idea of aiming high and one day reaching the stars.

Or maybe it was because when he was rejected by a woman, he saw fit to kill them. It was almost as though he was waiting for an excuse to. *If I choose to love her back, it can only end well. I'm not sure that's what I want.* Olivia chose to read between the lines of his riddles and came to her own conclusions. Tanya cared for him, and he saw potential there, but he was scared that he'd never get to end her life. That settling down with her would mean that his killing days were over. The days of having killing power of the kind of women who had power over him in life would end.

But there was more to it. *I'll always be at home with Tanya.* He saw her as a place to go back to, a safe haven. Olivia thumbed back to her first mention in the book. Each of the women had a page that almost served as a profile. He'd stuck a photograph of them in there, along with their date of birth, their horoscope and their full name. But most importantly, he'd also noted their addresses. Olivia's heart pounded as she read over Tanya's address. Was it possible she still lived there?

"There's an address in here for Tanya Benson... she's the only one of his conquests still alive... or at least, I presume so. She has two previous entries in the book and there are no Polaroids of her in the drawer. I think... I think he might have run to her now."

"You really think so?"

"He said she feels like home to him. And he never allowed himself to invest in her... he was scared of settling down and having to give up his killing spree."

"Oh God."

"I know. It's bad. But it might just help us here. Can you check out this address while I read through the rest of the book?"

While McCarty was doing some research, Olivia continued her search. It was only when the pages suddenly became repetitive that Olivia paused her flicking. There was page after page of Caro's name, scrawled over and over like lines in detention. *Caroline, Caroline, Caroline...* it was anxiety inducing to say the least. Feeling unnerved, Olivia tried to turn the page, and was disgusted to find them stuck together. When she eventually pried them apart, the obsessive writings went up a notch.

*Caroline will be mine. Caroline will be mine. Caroline will be mine.*

She flicked the page again.

*She touched my arm today. I can still feel her fingers on my skin. I can't stop thinking about it. I'll never wash there again. Maybe I'll get a tattoo there. She never touches me. Something must have changed… maybe this is my time to make a move.*

Olivia didn't feel inclined to keep reading his obsessive thoughts about her cousin, but she forced herself onwards. She was getting close to the end of the book, but there were blank pages right at the back. She turned to the last pages where Nathan had written.

*She loves me… she loves me not… she loves me… she loves me not…*

*It's now or never. I guess I'll find out how she really feels. I hope she loves me. I don't want to say goodbye.*

Olivia's eyes swam with tears, but she didn't allow herself to release them. There was no denying it now. It seemed obvious to her that he'd written those words just before he hunted her down in the woods. He'd confronted her with an ultimatum. *Love me or die. Just like the others.* An icy chill ran down her back, but the book in her hands eased her mind a little. It was everything she needed.

"This… this is perfect," Olivia said. "It tells us everything we need to know… about all of the victims. We can get justice for them all… maybe even give other families some peace. And now we have a possible location too. Not to mention the fact that I've seen this handwriting before… I think I can get this to match up to the letter we found in Caro's hotel room. This is evidence in spades. The moment we find him, we'll have plenty to put him behind bars."

"Easier said than done, right?"

"Maybe. But this is a pretty solid route through his brain. When he feels threatened, he goes back to the place he feels safe. Like a child running to their mother when they've done something bad. He's emotionally stunted, but he still recognizes where he can go when there's nowhere else. I guarantee, he's on his way to see Tanya."

McCarty nodded. "Then we have to go too. Once the backup arrives, we'll head straight there. Let's catch this sicko."

# CHAPTER
# TWENTY-SIX

IT WAS ALL STEAM AHEAD AT NATHAN CALLOWAY'S apartment. While Brock coordinated with the responding officers already on their way, McCarty and Olivia continued to sweep his apartment for evidence that would build a case against him. While his creepy little notebook and collection of Polaroids connected him to Caro's death—plus a whole bunch of others—it never hurt to investigate further. They found when they opened his wardrobe that most of his clothes were gone, leaving bare hangers behind. They also checked his allotted parking spot in the lot and found that his car was gone.

"He must have had some foresight to pack some clothes... but if he left all of his trinkets behind then he couldn't have been in a stable state of mind. A rookie mistake," Olivia said. "Except he's not a rookie, is he? He's been doing this a long time."

"What would make him slip up so badly at this point?"

Olivia shrugged, shaking her head. "Any number of things. But I think the most likely thing is that he's feeling some kind of shame or anxiety about what he's done. It's like I said before, Caro was in his life for a lot longer than his other victims. Maybe he got attached in a way he hadn't before. And now that she's dead… maybe he almost wants to be caught. Because if we don't find him and put him away, he's going to have to find someone new to fixate on, and I don't think Tanya is really going to fit the bill. He just didn't have the same kind of obsession with her. Though it's interesting that he keeps going back to her."

"Hey, you guys should come and look at this," Brock said, peering around the bedroom door. "I found something."

Olivia followed him right away, curious to know what he might have found. In the kitchenette, Brock opened a cupboard under the sink and pulled out a clear plastic bag filled with devices. When Olivia got closer, she frowned.

"Burner phones?" Olivia asked. "What for?"

"There are labels on the back of them," Brock said quietly. Olivia fished into the bag and pulled out one of them. It had the name *Emma* written on a sticker on the back. It was an old model, probably around ten years old. When Olivia tried the power button, it unsurprisingly didn't turn on.

"I think there's one for each of the women he obsessed over," Brock said. "Tanya has a few in there. I guess because she's still alive."

"But why would he need a burner phone for each of them?" Olivia asked. "Why not just talk to them from his ordinary phone?"

Brock swallowed. "I think he was using the phones as some kind of virtual scrapbook. Or a filing system. There's nothing on these phones except texts to each of the women and pictures of them. He has explicit images of Tanya on her phones. I guess it's so that he can go back to them whenever he wants. No doubt the phones also have photos of the bodies on them. We would need to find a charger for some of the older ones. They're likely completely dead."

Olivia winced slightly at the choice of his words, but tried not to let them stick. She put the phone back inside the bag and pulled out Tanya's latest one. It was obviously newer, and almost fully charged when she tried the power button. The wallpaper on the phone was a photo of him and Tanya. It didn't look recent, the pair of them smiling and baby faced in comparison to their current selves. Olivia clicked on the photos app and then immediately wished that she hadn't. There were hundreds of naked photos of Tanya. She wasn't always aware she was being photographed, sometimes even sleeping in the images. When Olivia took a quick scroll upwards, she saw that there was a collection of videos too. She clicked them off, feeling like she had violated the woman's privacy. She had no doubt in her mind that Tanya had no idea she'd been so watched by her ex.

Olivia hesitated a moment before she clicked on the messaging app. As expected, there was only one thread of messages and it was between Tanya and Nathan. Olivia clicked on it and scrolled upwards to see the first messages. They were from a few weeks before.

**Nathan:** *Hey, it's Nathan. I've got a new phone. I thought I'd say hi.*

**Tanya:** *I didn't think I'd be hearing from you again.*

**Nathan:** *You know I can never really let you go.*

**Tanya:** *Then why don't you stop messing me around and commit to me? Is there someone else?*

**Nathan:** *It's complicated.*

The messages continued. Olivia scanned over them, wondering why Tanya would ever entertain Nathan's behavior. She wasn't an unattractive woman, and she clearly hadn't ever been Nathan's top priority. So why would she want him back anyway? If she had any clue of the things Nathan had done, she'd run a mile.

**Tanya:** *Can we meet?*

**Nathan:** *Soon. I want to, I really do.*

**Tanya:** *Then what's stopping you?*

*Nathan: I have some loose ends to tie up over here. I've got a lot going on. When I'm done, I'll come and see you, I promise.*

*Loose ends,* Olivia thought to herself. She knew he must be referring to Caro. It made her sick to think that was all she was to him. It was clear to her what Nathan had been doing. He was building bridges with Tanya again in case Caro rejected him. He was thinking ahead, making sure he had somewhere to go if things didn't go the way he wanted them to.

"He was planning his backup," Olivia said, trembling with rage. "He was buttering Tanya up in preparation for Caro telling him she wasn't interested. Which he knew would happen, deep down."

"Oh, Olivia..."

Olivia shook her head. "He's a monster."

She continued to read through the messages, her anger never letting up. She reached the end of the text chain. The messages were dated two days before.

*Nathan: Tanya... I need you. I need to see you.*

*Tanya: You know where to find me, baby.*

*Nathan: I'm on my way. I won't let you down this time, I swear.*

"He's definitely gone to find her," Olivia said, her heart racing. "He said he's ready to commit to her, to give her what she wants... but this is bad. Really bad. He's unstable now, more than ever, that much is clear. If he's not holding it together, he might try to hurt her. We can't let that happen."

"He's got a head start on us. It's a long drive to Oregon, but if he set off two days ago, he might get there soon," McCarty murmured.

"I wouldn't be surprised if he's been driving like a madman," Olivia said. "Not resting as much as he should, barely sleeping... he's a man on the edge. He must know he's running out of time, and it's scaring him. Maybe he wants to try and get one more kill in before his run is over."

"Then what do we do?" McCarty asked. "We can't catch up with him."

"We'll need to catch a flight. We might just about make it in time if we go as soon as possible." Olivia glanced at Brock. "I guess it's time to call in a favor at work."

After filling in her superiors on the case, Olivia and Brock secured access to seven tickets on the next flight out to Oregon for Olivia, Brock, McCarty and her team. It was hardly a high-speed chase when the flight would take them almost six hours, but to Olivia, it felt like one. Her heart raced all the way to the airport, all through security and through the flight. Brock advised her to get some sleep while they were traveling, but even though Olivia tried, her thumping heart kept her awake. It was impossible to shake off everything that had happened, all that she'd learned. Nathan had been fooling the world for years. Playing the part of the good guy, the best friend, the non-threatening presence in the lives of so many women. None of them thought of him as a killer, as a creep, as their worst possible nightmare. Olivia wished she had been able to tell Caro sooner that she was being played. That her so-called best friend would be the one to end her life.

But instead, Caro had died in the dark, all alone.

She didn't realize she was crying until Brock reached out and brushed a tear from her cheek. She put her hand to her face and it came away wet.

"It's nearly over," Brock promised her gently. "And you did this. You've solved the case in record time. You followed your instincts and you're going to arrest the man who hurt your cousin. That's something to be proud of."

Olivia wiped at her face again. "I made some big mistakes... especially with Caitlin..."

"She'll forgive you, in time. And you'll forgive yourself. Caitlin knew herself that she looked guilty. I don't think she had any love in her heart for her sister. You had to consider her. She brought that on herself."

"But to accuse her... and Finn too..."

"Finn is a piece of work. If anything, I hope you've brought to light what an ass he is. Maybe Caitlin will finally see sense and dump him. And you were the only person to be honest with her. Don't you think that's what family should be about?

Looking out for one another instead of hiding all your problems in the shadows?"

Olivia wavered and then nodded. He was right. Her family had been broken long before she got involved. She was sure things would never be the same between them all again, but what was she really missing out on? Olivia knew how Caro must have felt—isolated and alone even in a crowded room. Where had they all been when she needed them? And now, in their time of need, she was the one picking up the pieces again. So why did she care so much if she couldn't fix it all this time? It wouldn't be the same without Caro, anyway. If Olivia closed her eyes, she could see Caro's smile, the kind of smile that lit up a dark room. She could hear her laugh, hear her quick-tongued jokes and smart remarks. None of them had understood her. They hadn't wanted to.

But they'd miss her now she was gone.

Olivia took a deep breath. She told herself that this was all that mattered now. Getting justice. Saving Tanya's life, too. They'd called ahead to tell Tanya to go somewhere safe, but she had thought it was a prank call and put the phone down. They just had to hope that they could get to her before Nathan did. They didn't know for sure what he would do, but it couldn't be anything good.

Olivia refused to let him hurt anyone else. All those women had meant something to someone. And just because they'd never loved Nathan, a cruel and twisted monster, they'd ended up dead. It was so unfair that Olivia had to dig her nails into her palm to stop her own rage. She couldn't bear to let it continue for another minute.

Nathan Calloway was going down.

# CHAPTER TWENTY-SEVEN

THE RACE WAS ON. FROM THE MOMENT THEY GOT OFF THE plane, Olivia, McCarty and Brock were on high alert, calling the local authorities ahead of their arrival for assistance and desperately trying to get to Tanya before anything bad happened. Olivia tried to call her again, but when she didn't pick up, Olivia switched her efforts to getting to her as fast as possible. The worst part was they had no idea of Nathan's true intentions or how quickly he'd arrive there. It had been sensible, in some ways, for him to take his car instead of flying. He'd be much more likely to slip by unnoticed. And now they had to work against the clock to make sure he didn't arrive at his destination and kill his on-off beau.

They were closing in fast on the location given in the journal, but it wasn't fast enough for Olivia's liking. She hated the idea of anyone else getting hurt. They knew Nathan no longer had his trusty hammer, but he could be armed with just about anything. He had no previous criminal record, so there was every chance he'd gotten his hands on a gun.

He'd already killed eleven women.

He could kill one more.

The tactical van hurtled onto Tanya's street and the team readied themselves to take action. When Olivia saw that the car registered to Nathan was in the driveway, Olivia knew they were too late. They'd need to deal with him here and now.

"Everyone needs to be ready," she said. "He's here."

As the car came to a halt, they all hurtled out of the vehicle, closing in on the property. Inside seemed quiet, the curtains pulled across to hide anything happening within. McCarty's eyes met Olivia's.

"It's a federal case now. You should be the one to get us in there," McCarty said, nerves in her eyes. Olivia shook her head firmly.

"No. This is your case. Lead the way."

McCarty didn't second guess herself a second time. With a curt nod, she brought her guys forward to the door. She rapped three times on the door.

"Nathan Calloway. Open up! Police!"

Backup was arriving from the local police, crowding the street with cop cars. Olivia held her breath, hoping Nathan might just hand himself over. But when she heard the distinct sound of a door opening, she nodded to the back of the property.

"He's out the back! Go!"

They fanned out around the sides of the houses, Olivia and Brock taking one side while McCarty and her deputy took the other. Olivia ran harder than she had ever run before. There was no chance in hell she was letting him get away from them.

As they came out the other side of the property, Olivia spotted a gate leading into an alley behind the house. It was just banging closed. She propelled herself toward it, allowing the rest to follow behind as she followed a retreating figure down the way.

"Stop where you are!" Olivia shouted, but Nathan didn't slow. But his lumbering figure stood no chance against a police squad and two FBI agents. By the time he was making it out into the street again, Olivia was almost on him.

"Hands above your head!" she cried, but he still didn't stop. He glanced once over his shoulder, fear written all over his reddened face. *How does it feel to be the prey for once?* Olivia thought viciously.

"Stop or we will shoot you down!" McCarty cried. "It's over!"

Nathan finally slowed and turned. He had a knife in his hand. It was slick with blood. Olivia's heart seized.

"Someone go back and check on Tanya!" she cried. "I think she might be injured."

But then Olivia saw Nathan raising the knife to his wrist. There were several small slashes on his skin, though not deep enough to cause any damage. He had tried to take himself out before the police could get to him. Olivia's heart surged with anger. She wasn't going to allow him to get out of it so easily.

She was half his size, but she felt like she had the strength of a bull as she rushed him. She knocked the knife from his hand before he could make another incision, butting her shoulder into his. He recoiled a little and she restrained his wrists behind his back, panting hard. McCarty rushed to her aid, clipping his hands behind his back with handcuffs. Olivia felt blood from Nathan's wrists soaking her hands, but she knew he'd survive. The worst ones always did. The cuts weren't nearly deep enough. It was like he hadn't really tried, too afraid to do to himself what he'd done to so many others. She rounded him to look him in the eye, knowing what he was responsible for. He sickened her to her core.

"I hope it was all worth it," she snarled. "You're never seeing outside of a prison cell again."

There was a look of defeat in Nathan's eyes. He didn't say a word as he was carted away. Olivia stayed standing in the street, wishing she felt joyous at how it had all ended. But all she felt was misery. It wasn't a victory. She didn't feel like a winner when she'd lost so much. All because of a man like Nathan.

And she'd never be the same again.

# CHAPTER TWENTY-EIGHT

NATHAN CALLOWAY LOOKED SMALL SITTING ACROSS FROM Olivia, McCarty and Brock in the interrogation room. It wasn't a sight Olivia expected to see often when facing off with a killer, but on the rare occasions where it did happen, there was usually a good reason. Despite his stocky build, Nathan was shrinking into himself, as if shriveling up in guilt, like he regretted some of what he had done. But Olivia didn't have a shred of sympathy for him. Sitting across from him, knowing what he'd done, was a new kind of torture for her. How was it possible that he felt guilty when he'd killed over and over again, barely stopping for breath before moving on to his next conquest?

Even knowing that he would be going to prison wasn't enough for her. He deserved so much worse than spending the rest of his days in a cell. Eleven women were dead because of him and his fragile ego, because he couldn't stand the fact that he was undesirable to them. The thought made Olivia feel sick to her stomach. She had faced plenty of rejections in her own lifetime, but it had never ended with her going on a killing spree. Worse still, he'd made his first kill on a fifteen-year-old girl. A child. Someone who didn't even know what love was yet. She'd never get to find out.

And neither would Caro.

Olivia clenched her fists beneath the table. She couldn't allow Nathan to see just how deeply he'd wounded her. He didn't realize yet what this case meant to her, how it had become so personal even though she told herself not to let her emotions get in the way. The pain and suffering he had caused would be never-ending. Eleven families broken by grief too intense to describe. Eleven families with a gaping hole in the middle. Eleven families that would suffer every day, every birthday, every Christmas, with vital parts of their mechanisms missing. Did Nathan ever consider that before he killed a person? Did he ever think of anyone but himself?

Of course not.

Olivia was glad that McCarty was there to take the lead. She wanted to hear Nathan out, to see the case through to the end considering what she'd been through to get there, but she knew the moment she opened her mouth to speak, she was going to say things that she shouldn't. She was a professional at heart, and most of the time she was able to keep her emotions well in check, but that was before Nathan had messed with her family. This wasn't work. It was personal. This time, she couldn't separate the two.

"You are about to be charged with eleven counts of murder," McCarty said, her voice cool as ice. Brock's knee nudged Olivia's beneath the table and her breathing steadied a little. She was glad to have him beside her. "We found evidence in your bedroom of your obsessions with Caroline Knight and ten other women, who you ultimately murdered and then photographed the evidence. We also found your journal which details a lot of the things that you did in vague detail. Most recently, you killed Caroline Knight by striking her on the back of the head with a blunt hammer, the same hammer we think you used to kill the other women. Is this correct?"

Nathan swallowed, his throat bobbing. He didn't look any of them in the eye, like he wasn't capable of facing them now. "Yes."

"And then you hid the hammer under the tree where she told you she left a time capsule years ago. You decided to end your killing spree and run away to the safety of Tanya's home to start a life with her. Is that right?"

Nathan wavered. "Yes."

"Why?"

There was a long silence. McCarty leaned forward, her eyes ablaze.

"I asked you *why.*"

Nathan's lip trembled a little. "I… I don't know."

"Yes you do. You made that choice over and over again. Why did you do it?"

Nathan sniffed, still unresponsive. Olivia watched as his ugly face changed into a mournful grimace. "I… I didn't mean to do it the first time. My dad liked to tinker around in the shed in our backyard. I used to hang out there with my friends. I was in love with a girl from my class, and I invited her over because I wanted to… I wanted to be with her. I thought she might want to be with me too. The first time around… I tried to kiss her and she drew away from me. Like she was disgusted with me. Like I was *nothing*. She wasn't cruel, but I was embarrassed and hurt. She said she wanted to leave, but I didn't want her to go… I thought she might tell our friends what had happened, and they would all know that I was rejected. I couldn't stand the thought. Nothing in the world felt worse to me. And so I… I hit her. I picked up my dad's hammer and I hit her. I don't think I did it very hard… I didn't know she would die."

"You hit a girl with a hammer and didn't expect there to be consequences? You were sixteen years old. You knew, don't lie,"

Brock said. Nathan was sweating, an awful odor emitting from his body as he did.

"I... I didn't think at the time. I just went off my impulses and hit her once. I struck her cheek. She started to scream. She called me... she called me awful things. And I thought she was going to tell someone. She was screaming so loud, I thought our neighbors would hear and come running. I knew I'd be in trouble. So I had to hit her again. On the back of her head. And she went quiet. I... I meant to hit her, I don't want to deny that now. I don't see the point when you know it's not the truth. But I didn't mean for her to die."

"And the other ten times?" McCarty asked, raising an eyebrow. Nathan whimpered, staring into his lap.

"It changed me. I just... I was never the same. I had to take her body away and make it look like someone else did it. I took her away from the house in the middle of the night and found somewhere to leave her. I took a picture of her because... she was so beautiful. Even after what I did. And I wanted to remember her. I thought maybe the reminder would stop me from wanting to do it again, that maybe I'd learn my lesson. But I kept looking back at that photo at nighttime. And I started to feel... like I had done the right thing. She didn't want me. She made me feel small. And I wanted to feel big. Powerful. It takes power to kill someone."

His eyes darkened and his whimpering stopped. It was almost as though he'd reminded himself of who he was and why he did what he did. Now, there was no trace of remorse in his piercing blue eyes. There was only evil.

"The second time was easier. After the first body was found, I was too scared to do it for a while. But I moved away from home and I realized that I was living somewhere where no one knew my name or where I came from. If a girl turned up dead in the middle of the night, no fingers would point in my direction. It started to feel more plausible to do it again, if I needed to. And the thought comforted me. Knowing what I was capable of, knowing that I could use that power again if someone made me feel unworthy. I decided to start trying to talk to women, to see where it would take me. I figured I would either get to spend my life with a beautiful woman… or I'd get to kill one."

His voice carried no hint of emotion, not even malice. It was as if there was a deep void where his personality should have been. "I knew that it wasn't normal to fantasize that way, but I just kept telling myself that it wouldn't matter… I was going to have a beautiful girlfriend, and once I did, I wouldn't feel the need to kill anymore. But I still made preparations for either scenario, just in case. I started to realize that if I kept my hammer with me all the time, I would be ready if someone made me feel small again. And it just kept happening. I had a hard time meeting women, so I had to find creative ways to get into their lives. I would look for women in trouble at bars, or women struggling with their grocery bags. I'd tell those men to get lost or help the women take things to their cars. I found little ways to swoop in and be their heroes for a moment. And it worked as a way to get into their lives for a while. They all took to me very quickly because they saw that I was a gentleman. They saw that I was a nice guy. They all told me that I was different from other men. It made me feel good. So they'd bring me into their groups of friends and make me a part of it all. I thought that would be a good thing, constantly being surrounded by all these beautiful women… I thought that surely one of them would understand me and want me to be their boyfriend. But they never treated me right. All these women… they'd keep me around like some kind of pet. They'd be my friend and make me feel like I mattered to them… but when I'd tell them how I felt, they'd be so cruel. Some of them laughed me off. Some of them looked disgusted. And Caro… when I told Caro… she cried. As if it was the most awful thing she'd ever heard. She begged me to take it back. She said she didn't want to ruin what we had. But I was patient with her. I waited so long for her to love me. And she refused. And whenever it got to that point… when they told me they didn't want me, it felt easier to let them go than go forward."

"*Let them go?*" Olivia repeated through gritted teeth. "You didn't *let them go*. You *murdered them*. You smashed their skulls in and took photos of them like some kind of sicko."

Nathan's eyes snapped to Olivia. "I'm not a sicko. I just wanted to be loved. I bet *you* never had to worry about that, did you? A pretty woman like yourself? Do you have any idea what it's like to live in my shoes? To be rejected over and over again, like I don't matter at all in this world?"

"Oh, don't feed me that crap. I've read your sick little diary. You had so many opportunities to not do bad things, but you did them because they made you feel good. You had a chance to settle down and be in love with Tanya more than once and you rejected her. Because you wanted to keep killing. And in the end you couldn't even stop yourself from stabbing her, could you? Because you'd rather have her hurt to give you a chance to escape than face up to what you'd done. You wanted all of those women to suffer just because they never wanted you. How could *anyone* want you?"

"You're just like the rest of them," Nathan sneered, looking Olivia up and down in disgust. "Cruel and shallow. You took one look at me and made your mind up about me. Just like the rest of them."

"You're disgusting! And it has nothing to do with what you look like. I couldn't care less if you're the ugliest man alive. It's what's inside you that terrifies me. Did you ever consider that no one wants you because you're a cold-blooded killer? Because you're a *freak?*"

"Olivia," Brock said firmly. Olivia's heart was racing, tears stinging her eyes. Nathan clocked that she was crying and his face softened, confusion setting in his eyes. Olivia wrapped her arms around herself. Facing someone who had killed someone she loved was something new to contend with. She imagined all the people who she'd like to sit opposite and talk to. Adeline Clarke after she killed Jonathan. Her sister's killer. Everyone who hurt Brock when he was captured and tortured. She imagined what she'd say to them, how she'd tear into them and give them a piece of her mind. And now she had an opportunity. She glared into Nathan's eyes.

"That was my cousin you killed," she whispered, shaking in rage. "And you want me to feel sorry for you because you've never had much luck with the ladies? Do you realize how ridiculous that sounds? Plenty of people struggle to find love but they don't start killing people because of it. The world is a hard place to live in, but the rest of us just get on with it. I can't believe you'd try and excuse your behavior that way. What if that was your mother? What if you were never born because she rejected your father? What if I killed your father because he wouldn't love me? Huh?"

Nathan struggled for words. "I'm… I'm sorry."

"Tell me *why* you're sorry. I want to hear it. Because I don't think you have a shred of remorse inside you. How can you possibly be sorry when you've killed *over and over again* with the same damn results every time?"

Nathan hung his head, tears stinging his eyes. "It was different this time, I swear. After so much pain, I didn't really want to go on. I moved around a lot, trying to escape the things I'd done. I moved here five years ago and found a fresh start. I really, truly wanted Caro to love me. We worked together for two years and became friends. And she was different from the other women I'd met. She was the first one who treated me like a person. I knew from the start that she saw the good in me, that she actually wanted me around, even if not in the way I so desperately wanted. I fell for her so hard. I promise you that I loved her. But it backfired on me. I thought this time would be different. I convinced myself that it had to be. I really thought she would tell me she felt the same…"

"Then why the backup plan with Tanya Benson?" McCarty asked, her arms folded. "You still kept her on the back burner, didn't you? Because deep down you suspected that you'd kill Caro too."

Nathan shrugged helplessly. "I don't know… I don't think it's quite the same. It was a habit, I guess? This has been my life for over fifteen years. I don't know how else to be. It's like instinct now. But I was so desperate not to need the backup plan. I made it five years without a single kill. I thought I was different now, that I'd cured my impulses. I thought that it would finally be over… that she'd love me and I wouldn't have to carry on the way I was going. I'd finally have the beautiful girl, the one everyone wanted. But it… it didn't work out that way."

"What happened?" McCarty asked, her voice level and emotionless. She was keeping the interview back on track after a rocky middle. Olivia sat back, waiting for an answer. She knew she had to keep quiet if she wanted answers, even though her rage bubbled underneath the surface. Nathan sniffed.

"I knew she was heading to the lake house for the weekend. It wasn't often I could really get her alone. She was always surrounded by other men, or Eddie was there keeping an eye on her. But she said that she would be on her own to visit family. So I decided to try my luck. She had told me about her special tree in the woods, so it was just a case of finding it and waiting there for her. I figured she'd come at some point. I watched from a distance as she was enjoying time with her family... and then she started to walk away into the trees. And I knew it was about time."

Olivia shuddered, unable to stop herself. All the time she had been sitting laughing with Caro by the lake, thinking they were having a good time, Nathan was waiting out there in the trees like some kind of predator. How had she not known that they were being watched? How had she not felt a tingle on the back of her neck, fear like no other with a premonition of what was about to happen? If only she had known. If only she had considered the worst-case scenario waiting for them that night...

"I had to bide my time. She was talking to someone on the phone... I didn't want to startle her. I knew better than to risk that after all the times women have screamed when I've tried to talk to them. She was shocked when I showed up. She wanted to know why I was there, and I think she was uncomfortable because she wasn't her usual warm self with me. I guess I freaked her out a bit by showing up out of the blue, but I had to speak to her. I couldn't keep my feelings to myself any longer. I started to tell her everything... and I watched her face change. I knew before I was done that I wasn't going to get the result that I wanted. At least she tried to be nice about it at first. She said she didn't have feelings for me... or for anyone, for that matter, but I figured she was just trying to soften the blow. And she said she didn't want a relationship, not even with Anthony, who was always who I saw as my biggest competition. She took to him in a way she didn't with others, an obsession of her own, I suppose. But she told me that if she ever managed to lock him down, she'd soon grow bored of him too. She claimed that the chase was the fun part, and she didn't see herself sticking with anyone for that long. She said she liked her freedom too much to ever settle down with anyone... but that she never saw me in that way anyway. Not even for a one-night stand. That was the worst part... because there were *so many men* she was willing to give her body to. But still she refused to let me be one of them. I told her if I could just show her... then maybe she'd want me. I said I wanted to kiss her, to prove it. Then she started crying. She said she never got a chance to have a real friendship because men always wanted to make it into something it wasn't. She was going on and on about Nick... I hated that guy. I always thought he was a threat to me and her, second only to Anthony. But it turns out she didn't want him either. Or anyone, really. She claimed to not want drama, but I thought that was laughable. Drama followed her everywhere."

Olivia scowled, but a nudge from Brock kept her even.

"Five years, I watched men throwing themselves at her feet, treating her like the goddess she was. But she didn't shoo them away. She lapped it up. So I couldn't understand why she was so upset when I told her how I felt. It was like she was offended by it. And the more she went on about it and how much she didn't want me, the angrier I felt." He took a few deep breaths. "I'd told myself that no matter the outcome, I'd let her go. She was different from the others... I thought I would just go to Tanya and try to be happy. It didn't have to end the same way as the others. I didn't need to kill her to be satisfied the same way anymore. But I just go into this space where I don't really know what I'm doing. I detach from myself until it feels like an outer body experience. It doesn't feel like I'm actually doing the things I'm doing. And while she was weeping and wailing I just... I got so mad. I heard her saying she was happy to stay friends, but she would never touch me, and that I had to move on." Nathan gritted his teeth. "I started to really lose it. All that time, she was sleeping around, giving herself to all those unworthy men, and yet she couldn't see me for who I am. She didn't even give me a chance. I... I don't remember grabbing her, but I must have done it because she was thrashing against me, telling me to let her go. And I panicked. All of a sudden, I was sixteen again and my first was screaming, and I knew that I'd never have a choice. It always ended the same way. She hit me first, though. Bruised me and my face. And that snapped me into action. Before I knew what I was doing, I hit her with the hammer. And she fell down, just like the rest. She died before she hit the ground." He began to tremble, covering his face with his hands. "I… I tried to wake her up. I know how to revive a person… I put my lips to her mouth and tried to breathe life back into her. But she wouldn't come back. And when I heard two voices arguing, I knew I was running out of time. I didn't expect there to be anyone else out there in the middle of the night, but I guess I didn't strike luck that day. And that's when I went into autopilot. I took her photograph like the others. I made sure she looked pretty in the pictures because she was so beautiful. My dream girl." He began to sob, his shoulders shuddering. "Why couldn't she just love me?"

Olivia wished she could smash her fist into his face. She had never had a desire to hurt someone before, but she hated Nathan with everything she had in her. It was the self-pity that made it so much worse. The way he expected them to feel sorry for him, like he was the one who had suffered. The faces of all the dead women swam in front of Olivia's vision, their bodies perfectly arranged in the Polaroids. They never stood a chance around him. And thinking of his lips touching Caro's, even to try and revive her… it made her feel sick to her stomach. A few more days and they would've found his DNA all over her. He hadn't been in the right mind to stop himself from leaving evidence everywhere. They were always going to catch him. But Olivia didn't need to wait. He'd left a trail of breadcrumbs for them this whole time.

"I thought if I was patient it might work out for me," he cried. "Five years of my life… gone."

"And now you'll spend the rest in prison for what you've done," McCarty pointed out. "None of us ever get what we truly want in life, Nathan. But we don't go around killing people because of it."

"I didn't ask for much," Nathan said, his teeth gritted. "I deserved a good woman. A beautiful woman."

"You complained about all of these *shallow women,* but you're just as bad," Brock snapped. "All you wanted was a trophy to hang on your arm, hoping that someday people would recognize that you must have had something of worth to be with them. You're so much worse than you even realize."

"You're wrong. I'm not shallow. I wanted other things too. Caro was everything to me. But she didn't realize what she was doing… she didn't realize how she ruined her own worth by giving herself away so freely. She should have chosen one man to be with. I could've given her so much. And all the rest of them… they tainted themselves. They all thought they were too good for me. But I was stronger in the end."

"You're right. You were much more powerful than the fifteen-year-old girl you killed. What a prize," Olivia hissed. "Preying on the weak doesn't make you strong. And punishing women for not wanting you doesn't give you power. It just makes you the scum of the earth."

Nathan set his jaw. "I can't go back. I can't change what I've done. But at least if I can't have what I want, then no one can. No man will ever touch Caro again. That's my justice."

"You deserve everything that's coming for you," Olivia said, standing up on trembling legs. "I hope your time in prison will make you regret what you've done. Then maybe you'll feel a fraction of the pain you've inflicted. I'm done with you."

Olivia left the room. And some part of her felt peace. She didn't need to sit and argue with a murderer anymore. She'd said her piece, but he was never going to change. That was the problem. Trying to teach a murderer the error of their ways would never work. They were beyond saving.

But it didn't do much to ease the pain. And now that it was over, it came washing over her like a tidal wave. It crippled her, clenching her stomach so hard that she had to squat down in an attempt to stop the pain. And then the tears came. She felt arms wrap around her as she sobbed—Brock. There on the floor of the police station, Olivia wept for all the things she couldn't control or change. For all the women who lost their lives because of their choices. But mostly for Caro. For the woman who deserved more time. More love.

More everything.

# CHAPTER TWENTY-NINE

TWO FUNERALS IN ONE MONTH. WHAT A DEPRESSING thought.

Olivia stood in front of her bedroom mirror, smoothing down her black dress and holding back her emotions. It had been a few weeks now since she helped close Caro's case, and it hadn't gotten any easier. Every time she thought of her cousin, she found herself unable to hold it together. She wasn't much older than Olivia was, and now she'd never get a chance to grow old, to fall in love, to buy a house. All the little things that people took for granted had been snatched straight out of Caro's hands.

And of course, Caro's life had been far from a fairytale. Her lifestyle certainly wasn't conventional. But everyone who had known her properly had seemed to think she was happy. Yes, she made choices that others thought were odd, and maybe she lived outside of the ordinary rules of society. But if it gave her a good life, then who were they to argue with that? She had made an impression and been loved widely. Olivia was sure that the church would be packed that day.

She was dreading the funeral. After flying out to Oregon, Olivia hadn't had much time to return to the lake house and face her family, and she had been glad for it at the time. But now she would have to see them again for the first time at Caro's service. She didn't want to bring up the bad blood on Caro's day, but she was certain things would be uncomfortable. She owed Caitlin an apology, at least. She chewed her thumb. It had been a wild time, back at the lake house. Everyone had said and done things they didn't truly mean. Olivia could only hope that the dust had settled enough for everyone to get through the day without too much drama.

Brock entered the room and Olivia offered him a sad smile, tears trapped inside her eyes. He wrapped his arms around her and kissed the top of her head.

"You look beautiful. Caro would've loved that dress."

Olivia chuckled quietly. She had thought so too. The black lace over the body of the dress was just racy enough to get away with, and Olivia had thought of Caro immediately when she'd seen it in the store. Classy, but just a little bit saucy. Olivia wouldn't have dared wear it to a different funeral, but it was a nod to her cousin—if she was watching from somewhere, at least she would feel understood by someone.

"I wish we didn't have to go," Olivia murmured. Brock kissed her again.

"I know. Funerals are the worst."

"I can't stand them. We've seen too many."

"Far too many," Brock agreed. "But we need to be there. She would've wanted it."

"Of course she would," Olivia said with a quiet laugh. "One last chance to be the center of attention. All of her admirers lined up in a row… it's her dream."

"This is going to be a very male-dominated funeral, isn't it?"

"Very much so."

"I'll stick close to you. I don't want anyone thinking I'm part of the fan club. I've only got my eye on one lady."

Olivia managed a smile, slipping her hand into Brock's. His lame attempt at humor was appreciated. Brock brushed his thumb over her knuckles.

"Ready?"

"I guess I have to be."

Olivia closed her eyes for the whole drive to the church. She was meeting her parents there, as well as the rest of her family. They'd decided to get there a bit early to show their support, especially after all the drama that had been present the last few weeks. It felt right to put it aside for the sake of one day and try to make everything right.

The family were gathered outside under gray clouds when Brock and Olivia arrived, hand in hand. Olivia approached with a hammering heart. She was relieved when Stephanie stepped forward to envelope Olivia in a hug.

"Olivia, darling. Our little hero," she cooed. "You solved Caro's case… we can't thank you enough."

"You got justice for my little girl," Uncle Mark said with a reserved sniff. "I'm so grateful to you."

"It was McCarty's case," Olivia said, shrugging off the compliments. "I shouldn't be taking the credit. And I couldn't do it without Brock, of course."

"Good man," Uncle Mark said, clapping Brock's shoulder. "It's been so terrible… I haven't known what to do with myself. But it's a comfort knowing that the person who did this is behind bars. It's something to hold on to."

Olivia nodded in understanding. Nothing could ever make what had happened better. She knew that well enough from Veronica's death. She recalled standing outside the church that day, her heart heavy, and knew that she understood better than most what her uncle was going through. And unlike him, she would be there if he needed her. His past mistakes didn't mean she would abandon him in his time of need. Solving the case was the first step. Mending family relations would be the second.

Because that was the problem with family— no matter what they went through, they would always be bonded. The love between them could be weak at times, but it was still there. Olivia knew better than to push that away. When all was said and done, they could only rely on one another.

Olivia caught Caitlin's eye. She'd noted Finn's absence right away and that was even more relieving than Caitlin's calm demeanor. Caitlin nodded toward the church pointedly and Olivia swallowed, following her into the building. She could hardly refuse to speak to her now after everything she had done.

The church was quiet, and their footsteps echoed around the room as they walked up to the altar. A huge photo of Caro smiling was framed by flowers. A row of offerings from her many admirers had been left beneath the photograph. Caitlin picked up a fluffy teddy bear with a quiet scoff.

"Still an attention seeker, even in death," Caitlin said, but there was no edge to her voice today. It was almost an affectionate joke. "What's she going to do with all this stuff now, huh? It's not like she can use it."

"I guess it makes people feel like they've done something," Olivia said. "Like they can give her something in her next life."

"There is no next life. And they didn't give her anything. All they had to do was protect her. That's what love is about, right? And none of them managed that," she said. Olivia could see her fingers digging deep into the teddy as if she was she was squeezing the life out of it. Eventually, she let go and placed it back on the altar.

"I don't feel like I should be here," Caitlin said. "I had no love for her."

"I don't think that's true," Olivia whispered. Caitlin sighed.

"I really hated her, Olivia."

"I know. But she was your sister. That counted for more than you think."

"I feel so… guilty. She… she did try with me. I have to admit that now. And I never wanted it. All I wanted was to be bitter and hate her. I'd look at her and see all the things I wanted to be. The things I'd never achieve. And yet I'm the one still standing here. That's crazy. Clearly it should've been the other way around."

"Don't be ridiculous."

"Don't act like you wouldn't swap us in a heartbeat. I know exactly how you feel about me. The sun always shone on Caro, and you were close enough to feel the warmth. You never had much time for me."

Olivia swallowed, a lump forming in her throat. "I'm sorry to have ever made you feel that way, Caitlin. And I'm sorry for… for everything. I'm sorry I accused you."

"I would have done the same in your shoes. You made me see myself as I am, Olivia. A cruel, cold-hearted—"

"Stop. Just stop," Olivia said gently. "You're not. You're not at all. Tensions were high and I said things I never should have. If anyone was cruel, it was me. I thought I was doing the right thing. I was willing to do anything to get answers for her. But I've always cared for you both. I still do. I just thought Caro liked me more."

Caitlin snorted. "Well, that makes sense. I don't have the warmest presence, do I?"

"Well, I just… you and Veronica always clicked back in the day. I never saw it as an us and them kind of thing… I just thought we were all friends." Olivia paused. "Then we grew up."

"Then we grew up," Caitlin repeated, her voice hoarse. Olivia watched as she reached out for the teddy bear again. But this time, she clutched it to her chest like a child, tears forming in the corners of her eyes. "It puts everything into perspective, doesn't it? Someone dying. It reminds you of everything you haven't done yet. All the things you missed out on when you had the chance. I should have… I should have done more. I should have tried to fix everything. I acted like a child for so long. Just because I never felt good enough. That wasn't on her."

Olivia wavered. "Well… you know what? I don't think that's entirely true. On a day like today, we're supposed to say that she was perfect. That she was loved all around and will be missed by everyone. But it wasn't true. She interfered in people's lives. She caused trouble for the fun of it. She hurt people's feelings because she could. I loved her… but investigating her case made me realize that I idolized her when I shouldn't have. I think you were probably as bad as each other."

Caitlin blew out a silent laugh. "Gee, thanks."

Olivia smiled. "No, I mean it. You hated all the things she couldn't change, and she made you suffer for trying to make her someone she wasn't. But that's just being human. We all suck sometimes."

"Some more than others. And by that, I mean me, not her," Caitlin murmured. Olivia chewed the inside of her cheek.

"You know… you might think she didn't realize how much you cared. But I think you should hold on to something."

Caitlin sniffed. "Yeah? What's that then?"

"When she thought she was in trouble, she called you first. She went to you in the middle of the night when she was afraid. That counts for something."

Caitlin's lip wobbled. "And yet the night she died… I couldn't do anything. I didn't hear her. I wasn't far away and I didn't even know what happened. I should have saved her…"

"I don't think any of us could ever have known. There was nothing we could have done," Olivia whispered. As Caitlin began to cry, Olivia pulled her into a hug and held her. After everything, she was glad that she could at least comfort her. They'd both seen the worst of each other that week. But now, they could hold on to one another.

They were all they had left.

When Caitlin eventually pulled away, she was glassy-eyed, but she looked like her load had lightened a little. She sniffed and looked at Caro's photograph again.

"You'll be glad to know that I ditched Finn," she told the photograph. "I packed his bags in the middle of the night and changed the locks while he was out. He cried like a baby and begged for another chance. I bet you cackled at that."

Olivia smiled sadly. She briefly put her hand on Caitlin's shoulder and left her at the altar to talk to her sister one final time.

The church was full to the brim. So much so that people were standing by the time they closed the doors for the service.

Olivia sat beside Caitlin and held her hand at her request. Olivia understood—Olivia was the one person in the room who truly knew the complicated feelings of a sister losing a sister. Caitlin wanted someone beside her who understood those feelings.

Olivia saw Eddie—Caro's bodyguard—with his wife in the third row, his head bowed in utter pain. Then there were all of the hotel staff, all of them comforting one another. There was family, close and distant, crowded in the pews. There were familiar faces and people Olivia had never seen before. All there to celebrate Caro's life. Olivia stood with them all and sang hymns. She listened to every touching eulogy, every tribute to the woman Caro was, or who they pretended she was. She didn't mind. She didn't need to hear about Caro's flaws. She wanted a reminder of how loved she was. Nathan Calloway had tried to redefine what love meant when he killed her, but everyone in the church proved how wrong he was that day. Loving someone was never about receiving love back. It didn't come with terms and conditions. She wished he could have seen that. If he had, then he would have saved the rest of the world from a lot of pain.

Leaving the church, there wasn't a single dry eye. Olivia found Brock waiting for her outside with an umbrella as rain now lashed down on their shoulders. Olivia found shelter with him and he kissed her gently.

"You okay?"

Olivia nodded. In fact, she felt better than she had in a long while.

"It was a beautiful service."

He smiled. "It really was. And the music? Caro would have loved it."

Olivia nodded, unable to speak. Grief had her in a chokehold yet again. But something in the corner of her eye distracted her from the feeling. Something that made her do a double take.

Standing in the graveyard was a man in a black suit, but he wasn't a funeral goer. He wore sunglasses over his eyes, and he had no umbrella. He didn't seem concerned about the rain, and though Olivia couldn't see his eyes, she felt his gaze on her. She stared back, wondering what the hell was going on. He held up a hand and beckoned her toward him. The sight made a shiver run down her spine.

"Brock… there's someone over there. In the graveyard. He's trying to get me to go over there."

Brock followed her eye line to where the man was standing.

"He looks shifty. Just ignore him."

But Olivia had a feeling she knew exactly who he was and why he was there. They had unfinished business with someone, and he was there to enact the final stage.

"We have to go to him."

"Are you crazy, Olivia?"

"If we don't, something bad will happen," Olivia said bluntly. "I'm certain of it."

Brock's expression hardened, understanding her meaning. He gripped her hand tighter.

"I'm coming with you."

"I wouldn't go without you."

As people streamed out of the church in droves, they crossed the wet grass to the graveyard. The man, seeing that they were coming, took something out of his pocket. A mobile phone. He turned the screen toward them as they approached. There was a familiar face grinning back at them. Olivia wanted to scream, but she kept her face stoic. Of course she couldn't even have one day to mourn her cousin. It would never be that simple.

Not while their nemesis still walked the streets.

"Hello," Adeline Clarke said, grinning. "Have you missed me?"

# AUTHOR'S NOTE

Thank you for reading *Whispers at the Reunion,* the thirteenth book in the Olivia Knight FBI Series. We eagerly anticipate your company on the next exciting adventure with our beloved duo in '*Fatal Lies,*' where the Gamemaster's grand finale will be revealed. After all the anticipation, the time for the final showdown has come, and we promise, it will be worth every moment of the wait!

Our goal remains to provide you with the perfect escape into a world of non-stop excitement and action with every book. However, we can't do it alone! As indie writers, we don't have a big marketing budget or a massive following to help spread the word. That's where you come in! If you love the Olivia Knight series, please take a moment to leave us a review and tell your fellow book lovers about our latest installment. With your help, we can continue to bring you more thrilling adventures with Olivia and Brock, and make our mark in the world of crime fiction.

Thank you for your continued support, and we can't wait to take you on more exceptional adventures with the Olivia Knight FBI series!

By the way, if you find any typos, have suggestions, or just simply want to reach out to us, feel free to email us at egray@ellegraybooks.com

Your writer friends,
Elle Gray & K.S. Gray

# CONNECT WITH ELLE GRAY

Loved the book? Don't miss out on future reads! Join my newsletter and receive updates on my latest releases, insider content, and exclusive promos. Plus, as a thank you for joining, you'll get a FREE copy of my book Deadly Pursuit!

Deadly Pursuit follows the story of Paxton Arrington, a police officer in Seattle who uncovers corruption within his own precinct. With his career and reputation on the line, he enlists the help of his FBI friend Blake Wilder to bring down the corrupt Strike Team. But the stakes are high, and Paxton must decide whether he's willing to risk everything to do the right thing.

Claiming your freebie is easy! Visit
https://dl.bookfunnel.com/513mluk159
and sign up with your email!

Want more ways to stay connected? Follow me on Facebook and Instagram or sign up for text notifications by texting "blake" to 844-552-1368. Thanks for your support and happy reading!

# ALSO BY
# ELLE GRAY

### Blake Wilder FBI Mystery Thrillers

*Book One - The 7 She Saw*

*Book Two - A Perfect Wife*

*Book Three - Her Perfect Crime*

*Book Four - The Chosen Girls*

*Book Five - The Secret She Kept*

*Book Six - The Lost Girls*

*Book Seven - The Lost Sister*

*Book Eight - The Missing Woman*

*Book Nine - Night at the Asylum*

*Book Ten - A Time to Die*

*Book Eleven - The House on the Hill*

*Book Twelve - The Missing Girls*

*Book Thirteen - No More Lies*

*Book Fourteen - The Unlucky Girl*

*Book Fifteen - The Heist*

*Book Sixteen - The Hit List*

*Book Seventeen - The Missing Daughter*

*Book Eighteen - The Silent Threat*

*Book Nineteen - A Code to Kill*

*Book Twenty - Watching Her*

*Book Twenty-One - The Inmate's Secret*

*Book Twenty-Two - A Motive to Kill*

# ALSO BY
# ELLE GRAY | K.S. GRAY

# ALSO BY
# ELLE GRAY | JAMES HOLT

**The Florida Girl FBI Mystery Thrillers**

*Book One - The Florida Girl*

*Book Two - Resort to Kill*

*Book Three - The Runaway*

*Book Four - The Ransom*

*Book Five - The Unknown Woman*

Made in the USA
Monee, IL
06 May 2024

58080024R10125